W9-BLK-812

TH1RTEEN R3ASONS WHY

TH1RTEEN R3ASONS
WHY
A NOVEL BY
JAY ASHER

razOr
bill

Thirteen Reasons Why

RAZORBILL

Published by the Penguin Group
Penguin Young Readers Group
345 Hudson Street, New York, New York 10014, USA
Penguin Group (USA) Inc., 375 Hudson Street, New York, New York 10014, USA
Penguin Group (Canada), 90 Eglinton Avenue East, Suite 700, Toronto, Ontario, Canada M4P 2Y3 (a division of Pearson Penguin Canada Inc.)
Penguin Books Ltd, 80 Strand, London WC2R 0RL, England
Penguin Ireland, 25 St Stephen's Green, Dublin 2, Ireland (a division of Penguin Books Ltd)
Penguin Group (Australia), 250 Camberwell Road, Camberwell, Victoria 3124, Australia (a division of Pearson Australia Group Pty Ltd)
Penguin Books India Pvt Ltd, 11 Community Centre, Panchsheel Park, New Delhi – 110 017, India
Penguin Group (NZ), 67 Apollo Drive, Mairangi Bay, Auckland 1311, New Zealand (a division of Pearson New Zealand Ltd)
Penguin Books (South Africa) (Pty) Ltd, 24 Sturdee Avenue, Rosebank, Johannesburg 2196, South Africa

Penguin Books Ltd, Registered Offices: 80 Strand, London WC2R 0RL, England

10 9 8 7 6 5 4

Copyright 2007 © Jay Asher
All rights reserved

Library of Congress Cataloging-in-Publication Data is available

Printed in the United States of America

The scanning, uploading, and distribution of this book via the Internet or via any other means without the permission of the publisher is illegal and punishable by law. Please purchase only authorized electronic editions, and do not participate in or encourage electronic piracy of copyrighted materials. Your support of the author's rights is appreciated.

The publisher does not have any control over and does not assume any responsibility for author or third-party Web sites or their content.

For JoanMarie

"Sir?" she repeats. "How soon do you want it to get there?"

I rub two fingers, hard, over my left eyebrow. The throbbing has become intense. "It doesn't matter," I say.

The clerk takes the package. The same shoebox that sat on my porch less than twenty-four hours ago; rewrapped in a brown paper bag, sealed with clear packing tape, exactly as I had received it. But now addressed with a new name. The next name on Hannah Baker's list.

"Baker's dozen," I mumble. Then I feel disgusted for even noticing it.

"Excuse me?"

I shake my head. "How much is it?"

She places the box on a rubber pad, then punches a sequence on her keypad.

I set my cup of gas-station coffee on the counter and glance at the screen. I pull a few bills from my wallet, dig some coins out of my pocket, and place my money on the counter.

"I don't think the coffee's kicked in yet," she says. "You're missing a dollar."

I hand over the extra dollar, then rub the sleep from my eyes. The coffee's lukewarm when I take a sip, making it harder to gulp down. But I need to wake up somehow.

Or maybe not. Maybe it's best to get through the day half-asleep. Maybe that's the only way to get through today.

"It should arrive at this address tomorrow," she says. "Maybe the day after tomorrow." Then she drops the box into a cart behind her.

I should have waited till after school. I should have given Jenny one final day of peace.

Though she doesn't deserve it.

When she gets home tomorrow, or the next day, she'll find a package on her doorstep. Or if her mom or dad or someone else gets there first, maybe she'll find it on her bed. And she'll be excited. I was excited. A package with no return address? Did they forget, or was it intentional? Maybe from a secret admirer?

"Do you want your receipt?" the clerk asks.

I shake my head.

A small printer clicks one out anyway. I watch her tear the slip across the serrated plastic and drop it into a wastebasket.

There's only one post office in town. I wonder if the same clerk helped the other people on the list, those who got this package before me. Did they keep their receipts as sick souvenirs? Tuck them in their underwear drawers? Pin them up on corkboards?

I almost ask for my receipt back. I almost say, "I'm sorry, can I have it after all?" As a reminder.

But if I wanted a reminder, I could've made copies of the tapes or saved the map. But I never want to hear those tapes again, though her voice will never leave my head. And the houses, the streets, and the high school will always be there to remind me.

It's out of my control now. The package is on its way. I leave the post office without the receipt.

Deep behind my left eyebrow, my head is still pounding. Every swallow tastes sour, and the closer I get to school, the closer I come to collapsing.

I want to collapse. I want to fall on the sidewalk right there and drag myself into the ivy. Because just beyond the ivy the sidewalk curves, following the outside of the school parking lot. It cuts through the front lawn and into the main building. It leads through the front doors and turns into a hallway, which meanders between rows of lockers and classrooms on both sides, finally entering the always-open door to first period.

At the front of the room, facing the students, will be the desk of Mr. Porter. He'll be the last to receive a package with no return address. And in the middle of the room, one desk to the left, will be the desk of Hannah Baker.

Empty.

YESTERDAY
ONE HOUR AFTER SCHOOL

A shoebox-sized package is propped against the front door at an angle. Our front door has a tiny slot to shove mail through, but anything thicker than a bar of soap gets left outside. A hurried scribble on the wrapping addresses the package to Clay Jensen, so I pick it up and head inside.

I take the package into the kitchen and set it on the counter. I slide open the junk drawer and pull out a pair of scissors. Then I run a scissor blade around the package and lift off its top. Inside the shoebox is a rolled-up tube of bubble-wrap. I unroll that and discover seven loose audiotapes.

Each tape has a dark blue number painted in the upper right-hand corner, possibly with nail polish. Each side has its own number. One and two on the first tape, three and four on the next, five and six, and so on. The last tape has a thirteen on one side, but nothing on the back.

Who would send me a shoebox full of audiotapes? No one listens to tapes anymore. Do I even have a way to play them?

The garage! The stereo on the workbench. My dad bought it at a yard sale for almost nothing. It's old, so he doesn't care if it gets coated with sawdust or splattered with paint. And best of all, it plays tapes.

I drag a stool in front of the workbench, drop my backpack to the floor, then sit down. I press Eject on the player. A plastic door eases open and I slide in the first tape.

CASSETTE 1: SIDE A

▶

Hello, boys and girls. Hannah Baker here. Live and in stereo.

I don't believe it.

No return engagements. No encore. And this time, absolutely no requests.

No, I can't believe it. Hannah Baker killed herself.

I hope you're ready, because I'm about to tell you the story of my life. More specifically, why my life ended. And if you're listening to these tapes, you're one of the reasons why.

What? No!

I'm not saying which tape brings you into the story. But fear not, if you received this lovely little box, your name will pop up . . . I promise.

Now, why would a dead girl lie?

Hey! That sounds like a joke. Why would a dead girl lie? Answer: Because she can't stand up.

Is this some kind of twisted suicide note?

Go ahead. Laugh.

Oh well. I thought it was funny.

Before Hannah died, she recorded a bunch of tapes. Why?

The rules are pretty simple. There are only two. Rule number one: You listen. Number two: You pass it on. Hopefully, neither one will be easy for you.

"What's that you're playing?"

"Mom!"

I scramble for the stereo, hitting several buttons all at once.

▶ ◀◀ ▶▶ ▌▌

"Mom, you scared me," I say. "It's nothing. A school project."

My go-to answer for anything. Staying out late? School project. Need extra money? School project. And now, the tapes of a girl. A girl who, two weeks ago, swallowed a handful of pills.

School project.

"Can I listen?" she asks.

"It's not mine," I say I scrape the toe of my shoe against the concrete floor. "I'm helping a friend. It's for history. It's boring."

"Well, that's nice of you," she says. She leans over my shoulder and lifts a dusty rag, one of my old cloth diapers, to remove a tape measure hidden underneath. Then she kisses my forehead. "I'll leave you in peace."

I wait till the door clicks shut, then I place a finger over the Play button. My fingers, my hands, my arms, my neck, everything feels hollow. Not enough strength to press a single button on a stereo.

I pick up the cloth diaper and drape it over the shoebox to hide it from my eyes. I wish I'd never seen that box or the seven tapes inside it. Hitting Play that first time was easy. A piece of cake. I had no idea what I was about to hear.

But this time, it's one of the most frightening things I've ever done.

I turn the volume down and press Play.

▶

. . . one: You listen. Number two: You pass it on. Hopefully, neither one will be easy for you.

When you're done listening to all thirteen sides—because there are thirteen sides to every story—rewind the tapes, put them back in the box, and pass them on to whoever follows your little tale. And you, lucky number thirteen, you can take the tapes straight to hell. Depending on your religion, maybe I'll see you there.

In case you're tempted to break the rules, understand that

I did make a copy of these tapes. Those copies will be released in a very public manner if this package doesn't make it through all of you.

This was not a spur-of-the-moment decision.

Do not take me for granted . . . again.

No. There's no way she could think that.

You are being watched.

II

My stomach squeezes in on itself, ready to make me throw up if I let it. Nearby, a plastic bucket sits upside-down on a footstool. In two strides, if I need to, I can reach the handle and flip it over.

I hardly knew Hannah Baker. I mean, I wanted to. I wanted to know her more than I had the chance. Over the summer, we worked together at the movie theater. And not long ago, at a party, we made out. But we never had the chance to get closer. And not once did I take her for granted. Not once.

These tapes shouldn't be here. Not with me. It has to be a mistake.

Or a terrible joke.

I pull the trash can across the floor. Although I checked it once already, I check the wrapping again. A return address has got to be here somewhere. Maybe I'm just overlooking it.

Hannah Baker's suicide tapes are getting passed around.

Someone made a copy and sent them to me as a joke. Tomorrow at school, someone will laugh when they see me, or they'll smirk and look away. And then I'll know.

And then? What will I do then?

I don't know.

▶

I almost forgot. If you're on my list, you should've received a map.

I let the wrapping fall back in the trash.

I'm on the list.

A few weeks ago, just days before Hannah took the pills, someone slipped an envelope through the vent of my locker. The outside of the envelope said: SAVE THIS—YOU'LL NEED IT in red felt-tip marker. Inside was a folded up map of the city. About a dozen red stars marked different areas around town.

In elementary school, we used those same chamber of commerce maps to learn about north, south, east, and west. Tiny blue numbers scattered around the map matched up with business names listed in the margins.

I kept Hannah's map in my backpack. I meant to show it around school to see if anyone else got one. To see if anyone knew what it meant. But over time, it slid beneath my textbooks and notebooks and I forgot all about it.

Till now.

Throughout the tapes, I'll be mentioning several spots around our beloved city for you to visit. I can't force you to go there, but if you'd like a little more insight, just head for the stars. Or, if you'd like, just throw the maps away and I'll never know.

As Hannah speaks through the dusty speakers, I feel the weight of my backpack pressing against my leg. Inside, crushed somewhere at the bottom, is her map.

Or maybe I will. I'm not actually sure how this whole dead thing works. Who knows, maybe I'm standing behind you right now.

I lean forward, propping my elbows on the workbench. I let my face fall into my hands and I slide my fingers back into unexpectedly damp hair.

I'm sorry. That wasn't fair.

Ready, Mr. Foley?

Justin Foley. A senior. He was Hannah's first kiss.

But why do I know that?

Justin, honey, you were my very first kiss. My very first hand to hold. But you were nothing more than an average guy. And I don't say that to be mean—I don't. There was just something about you that made me need to be your girlfriend. To this day I don't know exactly what that was. But it was there . . . and it was amazingly strong.

You don't know this, but two years ago when I was a freshman and you were a sophomore, I used to follow you around. For sixth period, I worked in the attendance office, so I knew every one of your classes. I even photocopied your schedule, which I'm sure I still have here somewhere. And when they go through my belongings, they'll probably toss it away thinking a freshman crush has no relevance. But does it?

For me, yes, it does. I went back as far as you to find an introduction to my story. And this really is where it begins.

So where am I on this list, among these stories? Second? Third? Does it get worse as it goes along? She said lucky number thirteen could take the tapes to hell.

When you reach the end of these tapes, Justin, I hope you'll understand your role in all of this. Because it may seem like a small role now, but it matters. In the end, everything matters.

Betrayal. It's one of the worst feelings.

I know you didn't mean to let me down. In fact, most of you listening probably had no idea what you were doing—what you were truly doing.

What was I doing, Hannah? Because I honestly have no idea. That night, if it's the night I'm thinking of, was just as strange for me as it was for you. Maybe more so, since I still have no idea what the hell happened.

Our first red star can be found at C-4. Take your finger over to C and drop it down to 4. That's right, like Battleship. When you're done with this tape, you should go there. We only lived in that house a short while, the summer before my freshman year, but it's where we lived when we first came to town.

And it's where I first saw you, Justin. Maybe you'll remember. You were in love with my friend Kat. School was still two months away, and Kat was the only person I knew because she lived right next door. She told me you were all over her the previous year. Not literally all over her—just staring and accidentally bumping into her in the halls.

I mean, those were accidents, right?

Kat told me that at the end-of-school dance, you finally found the nerve to do more than stare and bump into her. The two of you danced every slow song together. And soon, she told me, she was going to let you kiss her. The very first kiss of her life. What an honor!

The stories must be bad. Really bad. That's the only reason the tapes are passing on from one person to the next. Out of fear.

Why would you want to mail out a bunch of tapes blaming you in a suicide? You wouldn't. But Hannah wants us, those of us on the list, to hear what she has to say. And we'll do what she says, passing the tapes on, if only to keep them away from people not on the list.

"The list." It sounds like a secret club. An exclusive club.

And for some reason, I'm in it.

I wanted to see what you looked like, Justin, so we called you from my house and told you to come over. We called from my house because Kat didn't want you to know where she lived . . . well, not yet . . . even though her house was right next door.

You were playing ball—I don't know if it was basketball, baseball, or what—but you couldn't come over until later. So we waited.

Basketball. A lot of us played that summer, hoping to make JV as freshmen. Justin, only a sophomore, had a spot waiting for him on varsity. So a lot of us played ball with him in hopes of picking up skills over the summer. And some of us did.

While some of us, unfortunately, did not.

We sat in my front bay window, talking for hours, when all of a sudden you and one of your friends—hi, Zach!—came walking up the street.

Zach? Zach Dempsey? The only time I've seen Zach with Hannah, even momentarily, was the night I first met her.

Two streets meet in front of my old house like an upside-down T, *so you were walking up the middle of the road toward us.*

II

Wait. Wait. I need to think.

I pick at a speck of dry orange paint on the workbench. Why am I listening to this? I mean, why put myself through this? Why not just pop the tape out of the stereo and throw the entire box of them in the trash?

I swallow hard. Tears sting at the corners of my eyes.

Because it's Hannah's voice. A voice I thought I'd never hear again. I can't throw that away.

And because of the rules. I look at the shoebox hidden beneath the cloth diaper. Hannah said she made a copy of each of these tapes. But what if she didn't? Maybe if the tapes stop, if I don't pass them on, that's it. It's over. Nothing happens.

But what if there's something on these tapes that could hurt me? What if it's not a trick? Then a second set of tapes will be released. That's what she said. And everyone will hear what's on them.

The spot of paint flakes off like a scab.

Who's willing to test her bluff?

You stepped out of the gutter and planted one foot on the lawn. My dad had the sprinklers running all morning so the grass was wet and your foot slid forward, sending you into a split. Zach had been staring at the window, trying to get a better view of Kat's new friend—yours truly—and he tripped over you, landing beside you on the curb.

You pushed him off and stood up. Then he stood up, and you both looked at each other, not sure of what to do. And your decision? You ran back down the street while Kat and I laughed like crazy in the window.

I remember that. Kat thought it was so funny. She told me about it at her going-away party that summer.

The party where I first saw Hannah Baker.

God. I thought she was so pretty. And new to this town, that's what really got me. Around the opposite sex, especially back then, my tongue twisted into knots even a Boy Scout would walk away from. But around her I could be the new and improved Clay Jensen, high school freshman.

Kat moved away before the start of school, and I fell in love with the boy she left behind. And it wasn't long until that boy started showing an interest in me. Which might have had something to do with the fact that I seemed to always be around.

We didn't share any classes, but our classrooms for periods one, four, and five were at least close to each other. Okay, so period five was a stretch, and sometimes I wouldn't get there until after you'd left, but periods one and four were at least in the same hall.

At Kat's party, everyone hung around the outside patio even though the temperature was freezing. It was probably the coldest night of the year. And I, of course, forgot my jacket at home.

After a while, I managed to say hello. And a little while later, you managed to say it back. Then, one day, I walked by you without saying a word. I knew you couldn't handle that, and it led to our very first multiword conversation.

No, that's not right. I left my jacket at home because I wanted everyone to see my new shirt.

What an idiot I was.

"Hey!" you said. "Aren't you going to say hello?"

I smiled, took a breath, then turned around. "Why should I?"

"Because you always say hello."

I asked why you thought you were such an expert on me. I said you probably didn't know anything about me.

At Kat's party, I bent down to tie my shoe during my first conversation with Hannah Baker. And I couldn't do it. I couldn't tie my stupid shoelace because my fingers were too numb from the cold.

To Hannah's credit, she offered to tie it for me. Of course, I wouldn't let her. Instead, I waited till Zach inserted himself into our awkward conversation before sneaking inside to thaw my fingers beneath running water.

So embarrassing.

Earlier, when I asked my mom how to get a boy's attention, she said, "Play hard to get." So that's what I was doing. And sure enough, it worked. You started hanging around my classes waiting for me.

It seemed like weeks went by before you finally asked for my number. But I knew you eventually would, so I practiced saying it out loud. Real calm and confident like I didn't really care. Like I gave it out a hundred times a day.

Yes, boys at my old school had asked for my number. But here, at my new school, you were the first.

No. That's not true. But you were the first to actually get my number.

It's not that I didn't want to give it out before. I was just cautious. New town. New school. And this time, I was going to be in control of how people saw me. After all, how often do we get a second chance?

Before you, Justin, whenever anyone asked, I'd say all the right numbers up until the very last one. And then I'd get scared and mess up . . . sort of accidentally on purpose.

I heave my backpack onto my lap and unzip the largest pocket.

I was getting way too excited watching you write down my number. Luckily, you were way too nervous to notice. When I finally spat out that last number—the correct number!—I smiled so big.

Meanwhile, your hand was shaking so badly that I thought you were going to screw it up. And I was not going to let that happen.

I pull out her map and unfold it on the workbench.

I pointed at the number you were writing. "That should be a seven," I said.

"It is a seven."

I use a wooden ruler to smooth out the creases.

"Oh. Well, as long as you know it's a seven."

"I do," you said. But you scratched it out anyway and made an even shakier seven.

I stretched the cuff of my sleeve into my palm and almost reached over to wipe the sweat from your forehead . . . something my mother would've done. But thankfully, I didn't do that. You never would've asked another girl for her number again.

Through the side garage door, Mom calls my name. I lower the volume, ready to hit Stop if it opens.

"Yes?"

By the time I got home, you'd already called. Twice.

"I want you to keep working," Mom says, "but I need to know if you're having dinner with us."

My mom asked who you were, and I said we had a class together. You were probably just calling with a homework question. And she said that's exactly what you had told her.

I look down at the first red star. C-4. I know where that is. But should I go there?

I couldn't believe it. Justin, you lied to my mom.

So why did that make me so happy?

"No," I say. "I'm heading to a friend's house. For his project."

Because our lies matched. It was a sign.

"That's fine," Mom says. "I'll keep some in the fridge

and you can heat it up later."

My mom asked what class we had and I said math, which wasn't a total lie. We both had math. Just not together. And not the same type.

"Good," Mom said. "That's what he told me."

I accused her of not trusting her own daughter, grabbed the slip of paper with your number from her hand, and ran upstairs.

I'll go there. To the first star. But before that, when this side of the tape is over, I'll go to Tony's.

Tony never upgraded his car stereo so he still plays tapes. That way, he says, he's in control of the music. If he gives someone a ride and they bring their own music, too bad. "The format's not compatible," he tells them.

When you answered the phone, I said, "Justin? It's Hannah. My mom said you called with a math problem."

Tony drives an old Mustang handed down from his brother, who got it from his dad, who probably got it from his dad. At school there are few loves that compare to the one between Tony and his car. More girls have dumped him out of car envy than my lips have even kissed.

You were confused, but eventually you remembered lying to my mom and, like a good boy, you apologized.

While Tony doesn't classify as a close friend, we have worked on a couple of assignments together so I know where he lives. And most important of all, he owns an old

Walkman that plays tapes. A yellow one with a skinny plastic headset that I'm sure he'll let me borrow. I'll take a few tapes with me and listen to them as I walk through Hannah's old neighborhood, which is only a block or so from Tony's.

"So, Justin, what's the math problem?" I asked. You weren't getting off that easy.

Or maybe I'll take the tapes somewhere else. Somewhere private. Because I can't listen here. Not that Mom or Dad will recognize the voice in the speakers, but I need room. Room to breathe.

And you didn't miss a beat. You told me Train A was leaving your house at 3:45 PM. Train B was leaving my house ten minutes later.

You couldn't see this, Justin, but I actually raised my hand like I was in school rather than sitting on the edge of my bed. "Pick me, Mr. Foley. Pick me," I said. "I know the answer."

When you called my name, "Yes, Miss Baker?" I threw Mom's hard-to-get rule right out the window. I told you the two trains met at Eisenhower Park at the bottom of the rocket slide.

What did Hannah see in him? I never got that. Even she admits she was unable to put her finger on it. But for an average-looking guy, so many girls are into Justin.

Sure, he is kind of tall. And maybe they find him

intriguing. He's always looking out windows, contemplating something.

A long pause at your end of the line, Justin. And I mean a looooooong pause. "So, when do the trains meet?" you asked.

"Fifteen minutes," I said.

You said fifteen minutes seemed awfully slow for two trains going full speed.

Whoa. Slow down, Hannah.

I know what you're all thinking. Hannah Baker is a slut.

Oops. Did you catch that? I said, "Hannah Baker is.*" Can't say that anymore.*

She stops talking.

I drag the stool closer to the workbench. The two spindles in the tape deck, hidden behind a smoky plastic window, pull the tape from one side to the other. A gentle hiss comes through the speaker. A soft static hum.

What is she thinking? At that moment, are her eyes shut? Is she crying? Is her finger on the Stop button, hoping for the strength to press it? What is she doing? I can't hear!

Wrong.

Her voice is angry. Almost trembling.

Hannah Baker is not, and never was, a slut. Which begs the question, What have you heard?

I simply wanted a kiss. I was a freshman girl who had never been kissed. Never. But I liked a boy, he liked me, and

I was going to kiss him. That's the story—the whole story—right there.

What was the other story? Because I did hear something.

The few nights leading up to our meeting in the park, I'd had the same dream. Exactly the same. From beginning to end. And for your listening pleasure, here it is.

But first, a little background.

My old town had a park similar to Eisenhower Park in one way. They both had that rocket ship. I'm sure it was made by the same company because they looked identical. A red nose points to the sky. Metal bars run from the nose all the way down to green fins holding the ship off the ground. Between the nose and the fins are three platforms, connected by three ladders. On the top level is a steering wheel. On the mid level is a slide that leads down to the playground.

On many nights leading up to my first day of school here, I'd climb to the top of that rocket and let my head fall back against the steering wheel. The night breeze blowing through the bars calmed me. I'd just close my eyes and think of home.

I climbed up there once, only once, when I was five. I screamed and cried my head off and would not come down for anything. But Dad was too big to fit through the holes. So he called the fire department, and they sent a female firefighter up to get me. They must've had a lot of those rescues because, a few weeks ago, the city announced plans to tear the rocket slide down.

I think that's the reason, in my dreams, my first kiss took place at the rocket ship. It reminded me of innocence. And I wanted my first kiss to be just that. Innocent.

Maybe that's why she didn't red-star the park. The rocket might be gone before the tapes make it through the entire list.

So back to my dreams, which started the day you began waiting outside my classroom door. The day I knew you liked me.

Hannah took off her shirt and let Justin put his hands up her bra. That's it. That's what I heard happened in the park that night.

But wait. Why would she do that in the middle of a park?

The dream starts with me at the top of the rocket, holding on to the steering wheel. It's still a playground rocket, not a real one, but every time I turn the wheel to the left, the trees in the park lift up their roots and sidestep it to the left. When I turn the wheel to the right, they sidestep it to the right.

Then I hear your voice calling up from the ground. "Hannah! Hannah! Stop playing with the trees and come see me."

So I leave the steering wheel and climb through the hole in the top platform. But when I reach the next platform, my feet have grown so huge they won't fit through the next hole.

Big feet? Seriously? I'm not into dream analysis, but maybe she was wondering if Justin had a big one.

I poke my head through the bars and shout, "My feet are too big. Do you still want me to come down?"

"I love big feet," you shout back. "Come down the slide and see me. I'll catch you."

So I sit on the slide and push off. But the wind resistance on my feet makes me go so slow. In the time it takes me to reach the bottom of the slide, I've noticed that your feet are extremely small. Almost nonexistent.

I knew it!

You walk to the end of the slide with your arms out, ready to catch me. And wouldn't you know it, when I jump off, my huge feet don't step on your little feet.

"See? We were made for each other," you say. Then you lean in to kiss me. Your lips getting closer . . . and closer . . . and . . . I wake up.

Every night for a week I woke up in the exact same about-to-be-kissed spot. But now, Justin, I would finally be meeting you. At that park. At the bottom of that slide. And damn it, you were going to kiss the hell out of me whether you liked it or not.

Hannah, if you kissed back then like you kissed at the party, trust me, he liked it.

I told you to meet me there in fifteen minutes. Of course, I only said that to make sure I got there before you. By the time you walked into the park, I wanted to be inside that rocket and all the way up, just like in my dreams. And that's how it happened . . . minus the dancing trees and funky feet.

From my viewpoint at the top of the rocket, I saw you come in at the far end of the park. You checked your watch every few steps and walked over to the slide, looking all around, but never up.

So I spun the steering wheel as hard as I could to make it rattle. You took a step back, looked up, and called my name. But don't worry, even though I wanted to live out my dream, I didn't expect you to know every single line and tell me to stop playing with the trees and come down.

"Be right down," I said.

But you told me to stop. You'd climb up to where I was.

So I shouted back, "No! Let me take the slide."

Then you repeated those magical, dreamlike words, "I'll catch you."

Definitely beats my first kiss. Seventh grade, Andrea Williams, behind the gym after school. She came over to my table at lunch, whispered the proposition in my ear, and I had a hard-on for the rest of the day.

When the kiss was over, three strawberry-lip-gloss seconds later, she turned and ran away. I peeked around the gym and watched two of her friends each hand her a five-dollar bill. I couldn't believe it! My lips were a ten-dollar bet.

Was that good or bad? Probably bad, I decided.

But I've loved strawberry lip gloss ever since.

I couldn't help smiling as I climbed down the top ladder. I sat myself on the slide—my heart racing. This was it. All my friends back home had their first kisses in middle school. Mine was waiting for me at the bottom of a slide, exactly as I wanted it. All I had to do was push off.

And I did.

I know it didn't really happen like this, but when I look back, it all happens in slow motion. The push. The slide. My hair flying behind me. You raising your arms to catch me. Me raising mine so you could.

So when did you decide to kiss me, Justin? Was it during your walk to the park? Or did it simply happen when I slid into your arms?

Okay, who out there wants to know my very first thought during my very first kiss? Here it is: Somebody's been eating chilidogs.

Nice one, Justin.

I'm sorry. It wasn't that bad, but it was the first thing I thought.

I'll take strawberry lip gloss any day.

I was so anxious about what kind of kiss it would be—

because my friends back home described so many types—and it turned out to be the beautiful kind. You didn't shove your tongue down my throat. You didn't grab my butt. We just held our lips together . . . and kissed.

And that's it.

Wait. Stop. Don't rewind. There's no need to go back because you didn't miss a thing. Let me repeat myself. That . . . is . . . all . . . that . . . happened.

Why, did you hear something else?

A shiver races up my spine.

Yes, I did. We all did.

Well, you're right. Something did happen. Justin grabbed my hand, we walked over to the swings, and we swung. Then he kissed me again the very same way.

Then? And then, Hannah? What happened then?

Then . . . we left. He went one way. I went the other.

Oh. So sorry. You wanted something sexier, didn't you? You wanted to hear how my itchy little fingers started playing with his zipper. You wanted to hear . . .

Well, what did you want to hear? Because I've heard so many stories that I don't know which one is the most popular. But I do know which is the least popular.

The truth.

Now, the truth is the one you won't forget.

I can still see Justin huddled among his friends at school. I remember Hannah walking by, and the whole group stopped talking. They averted their eyes. And when she passed, they started laughing.

But why do I remember this?

Because I wanted to talk to Hannah so many times after Kat's going-away party, but I was too shy. Too afraid. Watching Justin and his friends that day, I got the sense that there was more to her than I knew.

Then, later, I heard about her getting felt up at the rocket slide. And she was so new to school that the rumors overshadowed everything else I knew about her.

Hannah was beyond me, I figured. Too experienced to even think about me.

So thank you, Justin. Sincerely. My very first kiss was wonderful. And for the month or so that we lasted, and everywhere that we went, the kisses were wonderful. You were wonderful.

But then you started bragging.

A week went by and I heard nothing. But eventually, as they always will, the rumors reached me. And everyone knows you can't disprove a rumor.

I know. I know what you're thinking. As I was telling the story, I was thinking the same thing myself. A kiss? A rumor based on a kiss made you do this to yourself?

No. A rumor based on a kiss ruined a memory that I hoped would be special. A rumor based on a kiss started a reputation that other people believed in and reacted to. And sometimes, a rumor based on a kiss has a snowball effect.

A rumor, based on a kiss, is just the beginning.

Turn the tape over for more.

I reach for the stereo, ready to press Stop.

And Justin, honey, stick around. You're not going to believe where your name pops up next.

I hold my finger over the button, listening to the soft hum in the speakers, the faint squeak of the spindles winding the tape, waiting for her voice to return.

But it doesn't. The story is over.

■

When I get to Tony's, his Mustang is parked against the curb in front of his house. The hood is propped open, and he and his dad are leaning over the engine. Tony holds a small flashlight while his dad tightens something deep inside with a wrench.

"Did it break down," I ask, "or is this just for fun?"

Tony glances over his shoulder and, when he sees me, drops the flashlight into the engine. "Damn."

His dad stands up and wipes his oily hands across the front of his greased-up T-shirt. "Are you kidding? It's always fun." He looks at Tony and winks. "It's even more fun when it's something serious."

Scowling, Tony reaches in for the flashlight. "Dad, you remember Clay."

"Sure," his dad says. "Of course. Good to see you again." He doesn't reach forward to shake my hand. And with the amount of grease smeared onto his shirt, I'm not offended.

But he's faking it. He doesn't remember me.

"Oh, hey," his dad says, "I do remember you. You stayed for dinner once, right? Big on the 'please' and 'thank-yous'."

I smile.

"After you left, Tony's mom was after us for a week to be more polite."

What can I say? Parents like me.

"Yeah, that's him," Tony says. He grabs a shop rag to clean his hands. "So what's going on, Clay?"

I repeat his words in my head. What's going on? What's going on? Oh, well, since you asked, I got a bunch of tapes in the mail today from a girl who killed herself. Apparently, I had something to do with it. I'm not sure what that is, so I was wondering if I could borrow your Walkman to find out.

"Not much," I say.

His dad asks if I'd mind getting in the car and starting it for them. "The key's in the ignition."

I sling my backpack over to the passenger seat and slide in behind the wheel.

"Wait. Wait!" his dad yells. "Tony, shine it over here."

Tony's standing beside the car. Watching me. When our

eyes meet, they lock and I can't pull away. Does he know? Does he know about the tapes?

"Tony," his dad repeats. "The light."

Tony breaks the stare and leans in with the flashlight. In the space between the dash and the hood, his gaze slips back and forth from me to the engine.

What if he's on the tapes? What if his story is right before mine? Is he the one who sent them to me?

God, I am freaking out. Maybe he doesn't know. Maybe I just look guilty of something and he's picking up on that.

While I wait for the cue to start the car, I look around. Behind the passenger seat, on the floor, is the Walkman. It's just sitting there. The headphones' cord is wrapped tightly around the player. But what's my excuse? Why do I need it?

"Tony, here, take the wrench and let me hold the flashlight," his dad says. "You're jiggling it too much."

They swap flashlight for wrench and, at that moment, I grab for the Walkman. Just like that. Without thinking. The middle pocket of my backpack is open, so I stuff it in there and zip it shut.

"Okay, Clay," his dad calls. "Turn it."

I turn the key and the engine starts right up.

Through the gap above the dash, I watch his dad's smile. Whatever he's done, he's satisfied. "A little fine-tuning to make her sing," he says over the engine. "You can shut it off now, Clay."

Tony lowers the hood and clicks it shut. "I'll see you inside, Dad."

His dad nods, lifts a metal toolbox from the street, bundles up some greasy rags, then heads for the garage.

I pull my backpack over my shoulder and step out of the car.

"Thanks," Tony says. "If you didn't show up, we'd probably be out here all night."

I slip my arm through the other strap and adjust the backpack. "I needed to get out of the house," I say. "My mom was getting on my nerves."

Tony looks at the garage. "Tell me about it," he says. "I need to start my homework and my dad wants to tinker under the hood some more."

The streetlamp overhead flickers on.

"So, Clay," he says, "what'd you come out here for?"

I feel the weight of the Walkman in my backpack.

"I was just walking by and saw you outside. Thought I'd say hi."

His eyes stare a little too long, so I look over at his car.

"I'm heading to Rosie's to see what's up," he says. "Can I give you a lift?"

"Thanks," I say, "but I'm only walking a few blocks."

He shoves his hands into his pockets. "Where you off to?"

God, I hope he's not on the list. But what if he is? What if he already listened to the tapes and knows exactly what's going on in my head? What if he knows exactly where I'm going? Or worse, what if he hasn't received the tapes yet? What if they get sent to him further down the line?

If that's the case, he'll remember this moment. He'll remember my stalling. My not wanting to tip him off or warn him.

"Nowhere," I say. I put my hands in my pockets, too. "So, you know, I guess I'll see you tomorrow."

He doesn't say a word. Just watches me turn to leave. At any moment I expect him to yell, "Hey! Where's my Walkman?" But he doesn't. It's a clean getaway.

I take a right at the first corner and continue walking. I hear the car's engine start and the crunch of gravel as the wheels of his Mustang roll forward. Then he steps on the gas, crosses the street behind me, and keeps going.

I slide my backpack off my shoulders and down to the sidewalk. I pull out the Walkman. I unwrap the cord and slip the yellow plastic headphones over my head, pushing the tiny speaker nubs into my ears. Inside my backpack are the first four tapes, which are one or two more than I'll probably have time to listen to tonight. The rest I left at home.

I unzip the smallest pocket and remove the first tape. Then I slide it into the deck, B-side out, and shut the plastic door.

CASSETTE 1: SIDE B

▶

Welcome back. And thanks for hanging out for part two.

I wiggle the Walkman into my jacket pocket and turn up the volume.

If you're listening to this, one of two things has just happened. A: You're Justin, and after hearing your little tale you want to hear who's next. Or B: You're someone else and you're waiting to see if it's you.

Well . . .

A line of hot sweat rises along my hairline.

Alex Standall, it's your turn.

A single bead of sweat slides down my temple and I wipe it away.

I'm sure you have no idea why you're on here, Alex. You

probably think you did a good thing, right? You voted me Best Ass in the Freshman Class. How could anyone be angry at that?

Listen.

I sit on the curb with my shoes in the gutter. Near my heel, a few blades of grass poke up through the cement. Though the sun has barely started dipping beneath the rooftops and trees, streetlamps are lit on both sides of the road.

First, Alex, if you think I'm being silly—if you think I'm some stupid little girl who gets her panties in a bunch over the tiniest things, taking everything way too seriously, no one's making you listen. Sure, I am pressuring you with that second set of tapes, but who cares if people around town know what you think of my ass, right?

In the houses on this block, and in my house several blocks away, families are finishing up their dinners. Or they're loading dishwashers. Or starting their homework.

For those families, tonight, everything is normal.

I can name a whole list of people who would care. I can name a list of people who would care very much if these tapes got out.

So let's begin, shall we?

Curling forward, I hug my legs and lay my forehead on my knees.

I remember sitting in second period the morning your list came out. Ms. Strumm obviously had an amazing weekend because she did absolutely no prep work whatsoever.

She had us watch one of her famously dull documentaries. What it was on, I don't recall. But the narrator did have a thick British accent. And I remember picking at an old piece of tape stuck on my desk to keep from falling asleep. To me, the narrator's voice was nothing more than background noise.

Well, the narrator's voice . . . and the whispers.

When I looked up, the whispers stopped. Any eyes looking at me turned away. But I saw that paper getting passed around. A single sheet making its way up and down the aisles. Eventually, it made its way to the desk behind me—to Jimmy Long's desk—which groaned as his body weight shifted.

Any of you who were in class that morning, tell me: Jimmy was taking a sneaky-peek over the back of my chair, wasn't he? That's all I could picture as he whispered, "You bet it is."

I grip my knees tighter. Jackass Jimmy.

Someone whispered, "You idiot, Jackass."

I turned around, but I was not in a whispering mood. "You bet what is?"

Jimmy, who'll drink up the attention any girl gives him, gave a halfsmile and glanced down at the paper on his desk. Again came the "idiot" whisper—this time repeated across the room as if no one wanted me in on the joke.

When I first saw that list, given to me in history class, there were a few names I didn't recognize. A few new students I hadn't met yet or wasn't sure I had their names right. But Hannah, I knew her name. And I laughed when I saw it. She was building quite a reputation in a short amount of time.

Only now do I realize, that her reputation started in Justin Foley's imagination.

I tilted my head so I could read the upside-down title of the paper: FRESHMAN CLASS—WHO'S HOT / WHO'S NOT.

Jimmy's desk groaned again as he sat back, and I knew Ms. Strumm was coming, but I had to find my name. I didn't care why I was on the list. At the time, I don't think I even cared which side of the list I was on. There's just something about having everyone agree on something—something about you—that opens a cage of butterflies in your stomach. And as Ms. Strumm walked up the aisle, ready to grab that list before I found my name, the butterflies went berserk.

Where is my name? Where? Got it!

Later that day, passing Hannah in the halls, I took a look back as she walked by. And I had to agree. She definitely belonged in that category.

Ms. Strumm snatched the list away and I turned back to the front of the room. After a few minutes, gaining the nerve to look, I snuck a peek to the other side of the room. As expected, Jessica Davis looked pissed.

Why? Because right next to my name, but in the other column, was hers.

Her pencil tapped against her notebook at Morse code–speed and her face was burning red.

My only thought? Thank God I don't know Morse code.

Truth is, Jessica Davis is so much prettier than I am. Write up a list of every body part and you'll have a row of checkmarks the whole way down for each time her body beats mine.

I disagree, Hannah. All the way down.

Everyone knows Worst Ass in the Freshman Class was a lie. You can't even consider it stretching the truth. But I'm sure no one cared why Jessica ended up on that side of your list, Alex.

Well, no one except you . . . and me . . . and Jessica makes three.

And a lot more than that, I'm guessing, are about to find out.

Maybe some people think you were right in choosing me. I don't think so. But let me put it this way, I don't think my ass—as you call it—was the deciding factor. I think the deciding factor . . . was revenge.

I tear the blades of grass out of the gutter and stand up to leave. As I start walking, I rub the blades between my fingers till they fall away.

But this tape is not about your motivation, Alex. Though that is coming up. This tape is about how people change when they see your name on a stupid list. This tape is about . . .

A pause in her speech. I reach into my jacket and turn the volume up. She's uncrinkling a piece of paper. Smoothing it out.

Okay. I just looked over every name—every story—that completes these tapes. And guess what. Every single event documented here may never have happened had you, Alex, not written my name on that list. It's that simple.

You needed a name to put down opposite Jessica's. And since everyone at school already had a perverted image of me after Justin's little number, I was the perfect choice, wasn't I?

And the snowball keeps a-rollin'. Thanks, Justin.

Alex's list was a joke. A bad one, true. But he had no idea it would affect her like this. This isn't fair.

And what about me? What did I do? How will Hannah say that I scarred her? Because I have no idea. And after people hear about it, what are they going to think when they see me? Some of them, at least two of them, already know why I'm on here. Do they see me differently now?

No. They can't. Because my name does not belong with theirs. I should not be on this list I'm sure of it.

I did nothing wrong!

So to back up a bit, this tape isn't about why you did what you did, Alex. It's about the repercussions of what you did. More specifically, it's about the repercussions to me. It's about those things you didn't plan—things you couldn't plan.

God. I don't believe it.

II

The first red star. Hannah's old house. There it is.

But I don't believe it.

This house was my destination one other time. After a party. An elderly couple lives there now. And one night, about a month ago, the husband was driving his car a few blocks away, talking to his wife on the phone when he hit another car.

I shut my eyes and shake my head against the memory. I don't want to see it. But I can't help it. The man was hysterical. Crying. "I need to call her! I need to call my wife!" His phone had disappeared somewhere in the crash. We tried using mine to call her back, but his wife's phone kept ringing. She was confused, too afraid to click over. She wanted to stay on the line, the line her husband had called her on.

She had a bad heart, he said. She needed to know he was okay.

I called the police, using my phone, and told the man I

would continue trying to reach his wife. But he told me I needed to tell her. She needed to know he was okay. Their house wasn't far.

A tiny crowd had gathered, some of them taking care of the person in the other car. He was from our school. A senior. And he was in much worse shape than the old man. I shouted for a few of them to wait with my guy till an ambulance arrived. Then I left, racing toward his house to calm his wife. But I didn't know I was also racing toward a house Hannah once lived in.

This house.

But this time, I walk. Like Justin and Zach, I walk down the center of the road toward East Floral Canyon where two streets meet like an upside-down *T*, just as Hannah described it.

The curtains in the bay window are shut for the night. But the summer before our freshman year, Hannah stood there with Kat. The two of them looked out, to where I am now, and they watched two boys walk up the street. They watched them step off the road and onto the wet grass, slipping and tumbling over each other.

I keep walking till I reach the gutter, pressing the toes of my shoes against the curb. I step up onto the grass and just stand there. A simple, basic step. I don't slip, and I can't help wondering, had Justin and Zach made it to Hannah's front door, would she have fallen for Zach instead of Justin a few months later? Would Justin have been wiped out of the picture? Would the rumors never have started?

Would Hannah still be alive?

▶

The day your list came out wasn't too traumatic. I survived. I knew it was a joke. And the people I saw standing in the halls, huddled around whoever had a copy, they knew it was a joke, too. One big, fat, happy joke.

But what happens when someone says you have the best ass in the freshman class? Let me tell you, Alex, because you'll never know. It gives people—some people—the go-ahead to treat you like you're nothing but that specific body part.

Need an example? Fine. B-3 on your maps. Blue Spot Liquor.

It's nearby.

I have no idea why it's called that, but it's only a block or so away from my first house. I used to walk there any time I had a sweet tooth. Which means, yes, I went there every day.

Blue Spot has always looked grimy from the sidewalk, so I've never actually gone inside.

Ninety-five percent of the time, Blue Spot was empty. Just me and the man behind the register.

I don't think a lot of people know it's even there because it's tiny and squished between two other stores, both of which have been closed since we moved here. From the sidewalk, Blue Spot looks like a posting board for cigarette and alcohol ads. And inside? Well, it looks about the same.

I walk along the sidewalk in front of Hannah's old house. A driveway climbs up a gentle slope before disappearing beneath a weathered wooden garage door.

Hanging over the front of the counter, a wire rack holds all the best candies. Well, they're my favorites anyway. And the moment I open the door, the man at the register rings me up–cha-ching–*Even before I pick up a candy bar, because he knows I never leave without one.*

Someone once described the man behind the counter as having the face of a walnut. And he does! Probably from smoking so much, but having the name Wally probably doesn't help.

Ever since she arrived, Hannah rode a blue bike to school. I can almost picture her now. Right here. Backpack on, coasting down the driveway. Her front wheel turns and she pedals past me on the sidewalk. I watch her ride down a long stretch of sidewalk, passing trees, parked cars, and houses. I stand and watch her image disappear.

Again.

Then I turn slowly and walk away.

Honestly, in all the times I've been to Blue Spot, I don't think I've heard Wally utter a single word. I'm trying to remember a single "hello" or "hey" or even a friendly grunt. But the only sound I ever heard him utter was because of you, Alex.

What a pal.

Alex! That's right. Yesterday, someone shoved him in the halls. Someone shoved Alex into me. But who?

That day, as usual, a bell jingled over the door as I walked in. Cha-ching! *went the register. I picked out a candy bar from the rack on the counter, but I can't tell you which one because I don't remember.*

I caught Alex to keep him from falling. I asked if he was okay, but he just ignored me, picked up his backpack, and hurried down the hall. Did I do something to piss him off, I wondered. I couldn't think of anything.

If I wanted to, I could tell you the name of the person who walked in while I searched my backpack for money. I do remember. But he was just one of many jerks I've run into over the years.

I don't know, maybe I should expose all of them. But as far as your story goes, Alex, his action—his horrible, disgusting action—was just an aftereffect of yours.

Plus, he's got a whole tape all to himself . . .

I wince. What happened in that store because of Alex's list?

No, I don't want to know. And I don't want to see Alex. Not tomorrow. Not the day after that. I don't want to see him or Justin. Or fat-ass Jackass Jimmy. God, who else is involved in this?

He threw open the door to Blue Spot. "Hey, Wally!" he said. And he said it with such arrogance, which sounded so natural coming from his mouth. I could tell it wasn't the first time he said it that way, acting like Wally was beneath him. "Oh, Hannah, hey," he said. "I didn't see you there."

Did I mention I was standing at the counter, visible to anyone the moment they opened the door?

I acknowledged him with a tiny smile, found my money, and dropped it into Wally's wrinkled hand. Wally, as far as I could tell, didn't respond to him in any way. Not an eye catch or a twitch or a smile—his usual greeting for me.

I follow the sidewalk around a corner, away from the residential streets, on my way to Blue Spot.

It's amazing how a town can change so much in one corner. The houses behind me weren't big or fancy. Very middle class. But they sit back-to-back with the part of town that's been slowly falling apart for years.

"Hey Wally, guess what?" His breath came from just over my shoulder.

My backpack was resting on the counter while I zipped it shut. Wally's eyes were focused down, just beyond the edge of the counter, near my waist, and I knew what was coming.

A cupped hand smacked my ass. And then, he said it.

"Best Ass in the Freshman Class, Wally. Standing right here in your store!"

There's more than a few guys I can picture doing that. The sarcasm. The arrogance.

Did it hurt? No. But that doesn't matter, does it? Because the question is, did he have the right to do it? And the answer, I hope, is obvious.

I knocked his hand away with a quick backhand swipe that every girl should master. And that's when Wally emerged from his shell. That's when Wally made a sound. His mouth stayed shut, and it was nothing more than a quick click of the tongue, but that little noise took me by surprise. Inside, I knew, Wally was a ball of rage.

And there it is. The neon sign of Blue Spot Liquor.

II

On this block, only two stores remain open: Blue Spot Liquor and Restless Video across the street. Blue Spot looks just as grimy as the last time I walked by it. Even the cigarette and alcohol ads look the same. Like wallpaper in the front window.

A brass bell jingles when I open the door. The same bell Hannah listened to whenever she came in for a candy fix. Instead of letting it swing shut behind me, I hold the edge of the door and slowly push it shut, watching it ring the bell again.

"Can I help you?"

Without looking, I already know it's not Wally.

But why am I disappointed? I didn't come to see Wally.

He asks again, a little louder, "Can I help you?"

I can't bring myself to look toward the front counter. Not yet. I don't want to imagine her standing there.

At the back of the store, behind a wall of see-through doors, are the refrigerated drinks. And even though I'm not thirsty, I go there. I open one of the doors and take an orange soda, the first plastic bottle I touch. Then I walk to the front of the store and pull out my wallet.

A wire rack loaded with candy bars hangs from the front counter. These are the ones Hannah liked.

My left eye begins to twitch.

"Is that all?" he asks.

I place the soda on the counter and look down, rubbing my eye. The pain begins somewhere above my eye, but it goes deeper. Behind my eyebrow. A pinching I've never felt before.

"There's more behind you," the clerk says. He must think I'm looking at the candy.

I grab a Butterfinger from the rack and place it next to my drink. I put a few dollars on the counter and slide them over to him.

Cha-ching!

He slides back a couple of coins and I notice a plastic nametag stuck to the register.

"Does he still work here?" I ask.

"Wally?" The clerk exhales through his nose. "Day shift."

When I leave, the brass bell jingles.

▶

I swung my backpack over my shoulder and probably whispered, "Excuse me," but when I moved around him, I purposely avoided his eyes.

I had the door in sight, ready to leave, when he grabbed my wrist and spun me around.

He said my name, and when I looked into his eyes the joking was gone.

I yanked my arm, but his grip was tight.

Across the street, the neon sign of Restless Video flickers erratically.

I know who Hannah's talking about now. I've seen his wrist-grabbing stunt before. It always makes me want to grab him by the shirt and push him until he lets the girl go.

But instead, every time, I pretend not to notice.

What could I do, anyway?

Then the jerk let go and put his hand on my shoulder. "I'm only playing, Hannah. Just relax."

Okay, let's dissect what just happened. I thought about it the entire walk home from Blue Spot, which is probably why I don't remember which candy bar I bought that day.

I sit on the chipped curb outside of Blue Spot, setting the

orange soda next to me and balancing the Butterfinger on my knee. Not that I have an appetite for anything sweet.

So why did I buy it? Was it only because Hannah used to buy candy from the same rack? And why does that matter? I went to the first red star. And the second. I don't need to go everywhere or do everything she says.

First his words—then his actions.

Statement number one: "I'm only playing, Hannah."

Translation: Your ass is my play-toy. You might think you have final say over what happens to your ass, but you don't. At least, not as long as "I'm only playing."

I tap one end of the candy bar, making it teeter-totter on my knee.

Statement number two: "Just relax."

Translation: Come on, Hannah, all I did was touch you with no indication that you wanted me to touch you. If it'll make you feel better, go ahead, you can touch me wherever you'd like.

Now let's talk about his actions, shall we?

Action number one: Grabbing my ass.

Interpretation: Let me back up and say that this guy had never grabbed my ass before. So why now? My pants weren't anything special. They weren't overly tight. Sure, they were slung a little low and he probably got a hip shot, but he didn't grab my hips. He grabbed my ass.

I'm starting to understand. I'm starting to see what

Hannah means. And that opens up a black hole in the pit of my stomach.

Best Lips. That was another category on the list.

Alex, am I saying your list gave him permission to grab my ass? No. I'm saying it gave him an excuse. And an excuse was all this guy needed.

It wasn't till that list came out that I even noticed Angela Romero's lips. But after that, I became fascinated by them. When I watched her give speeches during class, I had no idea what words came out of her mouth. I just watched those lips move up and down. Mesmerized when she said things like "slippery slope," which, behind her lips, exposed the underside of her tongue.

Action number two: He grabbed my wrist then put his hand on my shoulder.

You know, I'm not even going to interpret this. I'm just going to tell you why it pissed me off. I've had my butt grabbed before—no big deal—but this time it was grabbed because someone else wrote my name on a list. And when this guy saw me upset, did he apologize? No. Instead, he got aggressive. Then, in the most condescending way, he told me to relax. Then he put his hand on my shoulder, as if by touching me he'd somehow comfort me.

Here's a tip. If you touch a girl, even as a joke, and she pushes you off, leave . . . her . . . alone. Don't touch her. Anywhere! Just stop. Your touch does nothing but sicken her.

The rest of Angela was nowhere near as mesmerizing as

her lips. Not bad, just not mesmerizing.

Then, last summer at a friend's house, we played spin the bottle after a bunch of us admitted we were spin-the-bottle virgins. And I refused to let the game end till my spin landed on Angela. Or till her spin landed on me. When that happened, I pressed my lips, agonizingly slowly and precisely, against hers.

There are some sick and twisted people out there, Alex—and maybe I'm one of them—but the point is, when you hold people up for ridicule, you have to take responsibility when other people act on it.

Later on, Angela and I made out on her back porch. I just couldn't get enough of those lips.

All because of a list.

Actually, that's not right. You didn't hold me up for ridicule, did you? My name was in the Hot column. You wrote Jessica's name in the Not column. You held Jessica up for ridicule. And that's where our snowball picks up speed.

Jessica, my dear . . . you're next.

■

I pop open the Walkman and pull out the first tape.

In the smallest pocket of my backpack, I find the next tape. The one with a blue number three written in the corner. I drop that into the deck and snap the door shut.

CASSETTE 2: SIDE A

▶

Before Hannah's voice kicks in, there's a pause.

Step-by-step. That's how we'll get through this. One foot in front of the other.

Across the street, behind the buildings, the sun continues its fall. All the streetlamps are on, up and down the block. I grab the Butterfinger from my knee, the soda from beside me, and stand up.

We've already finished one tape—both sides—so stick with me. Things get better, or worse, depending on your point of view.

There's a trash can, an oil drum spray-painted blue, near the front door of Blue Spot Liquor. I drop the unwrapped Butterfinger into it, unable to imagine my stomach holding down anything solid, and walk away.

I know it may sound like it, but I wasn't completely alone the beginning of my freshman year. Two other freshmen, both featured here on Hannah Baker's Greatest Hits, were also new to the area. Alex Standall and Jessica Davis. And while we never became close friends, we did rely on each other those first few weeks of school.

I twist the top off my orange soda. It hisses and I take a sip.

With one week left of summer vacation, Ms. Antilly called me at home to see if I'd meet her at school. A little new-student orientation, she said.

In case you don't remember, Ms. Antilly was the guidance counselor for students with last names beginning A *through* G. *Later that year, she moved to another school district.*

I remember she was replaced by Mr. Porter. It was supposed to be a temporary position, but he's still at it. An English teacher as well as a guidance counselor.

Which is very unfortunate, as it turns out. But that is for a later tape.

An icy sweat breaks across my forehead. Mr. Porter? Does he have something to do with this?

The world around me tilts and spins. I grab onto the trunk of a skinny sidewalk tree.

If she had told me the real purpose of our get-together

was to introduce me to another new student, I wouldn't have gone. I mean, what if we had nothing in common? Or what if I thought we had nothing in common but she, the other student, thought we did? Or what if the opposite happened and I thought we could become friends but she didn't?

So many things could have gone so horribly wrong.

I press my forehead against the smooth bark and try to calm my breathing.

But the other girl was Jessica Davis, and she didn't want to be there any more than I did.

We both expected Ms. Antilly to spew a bunch of psychobabble at us. What it means—what it takes—to be a great student. How this school is made up of the best and the brightest in the state. How everyone is given the same opportunities to succeed if they're willing to try.

But instead, she gave each of us a buddy.

I close my eyes. I don't want to see it, but it's so clear. When rumors of Hannah's unexplained absence began spreading through school, Mr. Porter asked our class why he kept hearing her name mentioned in the halls. He looked nervous. Almost sick. Like he knew the answer but wanted someone to convince him otherwise.

Then a girl whispered, "Someone saw an ambulance leaving her house."

The moment Ms. Antilly told us why we were there, Jessica and I turned to each other. Her lips parted as if she wanted to say something. But what could she say with me sitting right there? She felt blindsided. Confused. Lied to.

I know that's how she felt because I felt the same way.

And I'll never forget Ms. Antilly's reaction. Two short, drawn-out words. "Or . . . not."

I squeeze my eyes tight, trying hard to remember that day as clearly as possible.

Was it pain on Mr. Porter's face? Or was it fear? He just stood there, staring at Hannah's desk. Through her desk. And no one said a word, but we looked around. At each other.

Then he left. Mr. Porter walked out of class and didn't come back for a week.

Why? Did he know? Did he know because of something he'd done?

And here, to the best of my memory, is what we said.

Me: I'm sorry, Ms. Antilly. I just didn't think that's why you called me in here.

Jessica: Me, neither. I wouldn't have come. I mean, I'm sure Hillary and I have things in common, and I'm sure she's a great person, but . . .

Me: It's Hannah.

Jessica: I called you Hillary, didn't I? Sorry.

Me: It's okay. I just thought you should know my name if we're going to be such fabulous friends.

And then the three of us laughed. Jessica and I had very

similar laughs, which made us laugh even harder. Ms. Antilly's laugh wasn't quite as heartfelt . . . more of a nervous laugh . . . but still a laugh. She claimed to have never tried matching up friends before, and was doubtful she ever would again.

But guess what. After the meeting, Jessica and I did hang out.

Very sneaky, Ms. Antilly. Veeeeeery sneaky.

We left campus and, at first, the conversation felt awkward. But it was nice having someone to talk to other than my parents.

A city bus pulls up to the curb in front of me. Silver with blue stripes.

We walked past my turnoff, but I didn't say anything. I didn't want to stop our conversation, but I also didn't want to invite her over because we really didn't know each other yet. So we continued walking until we reached downtown. I found out later that she did the same thing, walked past the street where she lived in order to keep talking with me.

So where did we go? E-7 on your map. Monet's Garden Café & Coffeehouse.

The bus door wheezes open.

Neither of us were coffee drinkers, but it seemed like a nice place to chat.

Through the foggy windows I see that almost all the seats are empty.

We both got hot chocolate. She ordered it thinking it would be funny. But me? I always order hot chocolate.

I've never ridden a city bus. Never had a reason to. But it's getting darker and colder every minute.

II

It doesn't cost anything to ride the bus at night, so I hop on. I move right by the driver without either of us saying a word to each other. She doesn't even look at me.

I make my way down the center aisle, buttoning my jacket against the cold, giving each button more attention than required. Any excuse to avert my eyes from the other passengers. I know how I must look to them. Confused. Guilty. In the process of being crushed.

I choose a bench that, as long as no one else boards, is situated between three or four empty seats all around. The blue vinyl cushion is ripped down the middle, with the yellow stuffing inside about to burst out. I slide over to the window.

The glass is cold, but resting my head against it helps relax me.

▶

I honestly don't remember much of what we said that afternoon. Do you, Jessica? Because when I close my eyes, everything happens in a kind of montage. Laughing.

Trying hard not to spill our drinks. Waving our hands while we talk.

I close my eyes. The glass cools one side of my overheated face. I don't care where this bus is going. I'll ride it for hours if I'm allowed to. I'll just sit here and listen to the tapes. And maybe, without trying, I'll fall asleep.

Then, at one point, you lean across the table. "I think that guy's checking you out," you whispered.

I knew exactly who you were talking about because I'd been watching him, as well. But he wasn't checking me out.

"He's checking you out," I said.

In a contest of who's-got-the-biggest-balls, all of you listening should know that Jessica wins.

"Excuse me," she said to Alex, in case you haven't figured out the name of the mystery man, "but which one of us are you checking out?"

And a few months later, after Hannah and Justin Foley break up, after the rumors begin, Alex writes a list. Who's hot. Who's not. But there, at Monet's, no one knew where that meeting would lead.

I want to push Stop on the Walkman and rewind their whole conversation. To rewind into the past and warn them. Or prevent them from even meeting.

But I can't. You can't rewrite the past.

Alex blushed. I'm talking an all-the-blood-in-his-body-rushing-up-to-his-face kind of blushed. And when he opened his mouth to deny it, Jessica cut him off.

"Don't lie. Which one of us were you checking out?"

Through the frosty glass, downtown's streetlamps and neon lights slide by. Most of the shops are closed for the night. But the restaurants and bars remain open.

At that moment I would have paid dearly for Jessica's friendship. She was the most outgoing, honest, tell-it-like-it-is girl I'd ever met.

Silently, I thanked Ms. Antilly for introducing us.

Alex stuttered and Jessica leaned over, letting her fingers fall gracefully onto his table.

"Look, we saw you watching us," she said. "We're both new to this town and we'd like to know who you were staring at. It's important."

Alex stammered. "I just . . . I heard . . . it's just, I'm new here, too."

I think Jessica and I both said something along the lines of, "Oh." And then it was our turn to blush. Poor Alex just wanted to be a part of our conversation. So we let him. And I think we talked for at least another hour—probably more. Just three people, happy that the first day of school wouldn't be spent wandering the halls alone. Or eating lunch alone. Getting lost alone.

Not that it matters, but where is this bus going? Does it leave our town for another one? Or does it loop endlessly through these streets?

Maybe I should've checked before getting on.

That afternoon at Monet's was a relief for all three of us. How many nights had I fallen asleep terrified, thinking of that first day of school? Too many. And after Monet's? None. Now, I was excited.

And just so you know, I never thought of Jessica or Alex as friends. Not even at the beginning when I would've loved two automatic friendships.

And I know they felt the same way, because we talked about it. We talked about our past friends and why those people had become our friends. We talked about what we were searching for in new friends at our new school.

But those first few weeks, until we each peeled away, Monet's Garden was our safe haven. If one of us had a hard time fitting in or meeting people, we'd go to Monet's. Back in the garden, at the far table to the right.

I'm not sure who started it, but whoever had the most exhausting day would lay a hand in the center of the table and say, "Olly-olly-oxen-free." The other two would lay their hands on top and lean in. Then we'd listen, sipping drinks with our free hands. Jessica and I always drank hot chocolate. Over time, Alex made his way through the entire menu.

I've only been to Monet's a few times, but I think it's on the street the bus is going down now.

Yes, we were cheesy. And I'm sorry if this episode's

making you sick. If it helps, it's almost too sweet for me. But Monet's truly filled whatever void needed filling at the time. For all of us.

But don't worry . . . it didn't last.

I slide across the bench to the aisle, then stand up in the moving bus.

The first to drop out was Alex. We were friendly when we saw each other in the halls, but it never went beyond that.

At least, with me it didn't.

Bracing my hands against the backrests, I make my way to the front of the shifting bus.

Now down to the two of us, Jessica and me, the whole thing changed pretty fast. The talks became chitchat and not much more.

"When's the next stop?" I ask. I feel the words leave my throat, but they're barely whispers above Hannah's voice and the engine.

The driver looks at me in the rearview mirror.

Then Jessica stopped going, and though I went to Monet's a few more times hoping one of them might wander in, eventually I stopped going, too.

Until . . .

"Only other people here are asleep," the driver says. I watch her lips carefully to make sure I understand. "I can stop wherever you'd like."

See, the cool thing about Jessica's story is that so much

of it happens in one spot, making life much easier for those of you following the stars.

The bus passes Monet's. "Here's good," I say.

Yes, I met Jessica for the first time in Ms. Antilly's office. But we got to know each other at Monet's.

I hold myself steady as the bus decelerates and pulls to the curb.

And we got to know Alex at Monet's. And then . . . and then this happened.

The door wheezes open.

At school one day, Jessica walked up to me in the halls. "We need to talk," she said. She didn't say where or why, but I knew she meant Monet's . . . and I thought I knew why.

I descend the stairs and step from the gutter up onto the curb. I readjust the headphones and start walking back half a block.

When I got there, Jessica was sitting slumped in a chair, arms dangling by her sides like she'd been waiting a long time. And maybe she had. Maybe she hoped I would skip my last class to join her.

So I sat down and slid my hand into the middle of the table. "Olly-olly-oxen-free?"

She lifted one of her hands and slapped a paper on the table. Then she pushed it across and spun it around for me to read. But I didn't need it spun around, because the first time I read that paper it was upside down on Jimmy's desk:

WHO'S HOT / WHO'S NOT.

I knew which side of the list I was on—according to Alex. And my so-called opposite was sitting across from me. At our safe haven, no less. Mine . . . hers . . . and Alex's.

"Who cares?" I told her. "It doesn't mean anything."

I swallow hard. When I read that list, I passed it down the aisle without a thought. At the time, it seemed kind of funny.

"Hannah," she said, "I don't care that he picked you over me."

I knew exactly where that conversation was headed and I was not going to let her take us there.

And now? How do I see it now?

I should've grabbed every copy I could find and thrown them all away.

"He did not choose me over you, Jessica," I said. "He chose me to get back at you and you know that. He knew my name would hurt you more than anyone else's."

She closed her eyes and said my name in almost a whisper. "Hannah."

Do you remember that, Jessica? Because I do.

When someone says your name like that, when they won't even look you in the eyes, there is nothing more you can do or say. Their mind is made up.

"Hannah," you said. "I know the rumors."

"You can't know rumors," I said. And maybe I was being

a little sensitive, but I had hoped—silly me—that there would be no more rumors when my family moved here. That I had left the rumors and gossip behind me . . . for good. "You can hear rumors," I said, "but you can't know them."

Again, you said my name. "Hannah."

Yes, I knew the rumors. And I swore to you that I hadn't seen Alex one time outside of school. But you wouldn't believe me.

And why should you believe me? Why would anyone not believe a rumor that fits so nicely with an old rumor? Huh, Justin? Why?

Jessica could have heard so many rumors about Alex and Hannah. But none of them were true.

For Jessica, it was easier to think of me as Bad Hannah than as the Hannah she got to know at Monet's. It was easier to accept. Easier to understand.

For her, the rumors needed to be true.

I remember a bunch of guys joking with Alex in the locker room. "Pat-a-cake, pat-a-cake, Baker's man." Then someone asked him, "Pat that muffin, Baker's man?" and everyone knew what was being said.

When the row cleared out, only Alex and I remained. A tiny wrench of jealousy twisted up my insides. Ever since Kat's going-away party, I couldn't get Hannah out of my mind. But I couldn't bring myself to ask if what they had said was true. Because if it was, I didn't want to hear it.

Tightening his shoelaces, and without looking at me, Alex denied the rumor. "Just so you know."

"Fine," I said. "Fine, Jessica. Thank you for helping me the first few weeks of school. It meant a lot. And I'm sorry Alex screwed that up with this stupid little list of his, but he did."

I told her I knew all about their relationship. On that first day at Monet's, he had been checking one of us out. And it wasn't me. And yes, that made me jealous. And if it helped her get over it, I accepted any blame she wanted to put on me for the two of them breaking up. But . . . it . . . was . . . not . . . true!

I reach Monet's.

Two guys stand outside, leaning against the wall. One smokes a cigarette and the other is burrowed deep into his jacket.

But all Jessica heard was me accepting blame.

She rose up beside her chair—glaring down at me—and swung.

So tell me, Jessica, which did you mean to do? Punch me, or scratch me? Because it felt like a little bit of both. Like you couldn't really decide.

And what was it you called me? Not that it matters, but just for the record. Because I was too busy lifting my hand and ducking—but you got me!—and I missed what you said.

That tiny scar you've all seen above my eyebrow, that's the shape of Jessica's fingernail . . . which I plucked out myself.

I noticed that scar a few weeks ago. At the party. A tiny flaw on a pretty face. And I told her how cute it was.

Minutes later, she started freaking out.

Or maybe you've never seen it. But I see it every morning when I get ready for school. "Good morning, Hannah," it says. And every night when I get ready for bed. "Sleep tight."

I push open the heavy wood-and-glass door to Monet's. Warm air rushes out to grab me and everyone turns, upset at the person letting in the cold. I slink inside and shut the door behind me.

But it's more than just a scratch. It's a punch in the stomach and a slap in the face. It's a knife in my back because you would rather believe some made-up rumor than what you knew to be true.

Jessica, my dear, I'd really love to know if you dragged yourself to my funeral. And if you did, did you notice your scar?

And what about you—the rest of you—did you notice the scars you left behind?

No. Probably not.

That wasn't possible.

Because most of them can't be seen with the naked eye.

Because there was no funeral, Hannah.

■

CASSETTE 2: SIDE B

In honor of Hannah, I should order a hot chocolate. At Monet's, they serve them with tiny marshmallows floating on top. The only coffee shop I know of that does that.

But when the girl asks, I say coffee, because I'm cheap. The hot chocolate costs a whole dollar more.

She slides an empty mug across the counter and points to the pour-it-yourself bar. I pour in just enough half-and-half to coat the bottom of the mug. The rest I fill with Hairy Chest Blend because it sounds highly caffeinated and maybe I can stay up late to finish the tapes.

I think I need to finish them, and finish them tonight.

But should I? In one night? Or should I find my story, listen to it, then just enough of the next tape to see who I'm supposed to pass them off to?

"What're you listening to?" It's the girl from behind the counter. She's beside me now, tilting the stainless steel containers of half-and-half, low fat, and soy. She's checking to see if they're full. A couple of black lines, a tattoo, stretch up from her collar and disappear into her short, cropped hair.

I glance down at the yellow headphones hanging around my neck. "Just some tapes."

"Cassette tapes?" She picks up the soy and holds it against her stomach. "Interesting. Anyone I've heard of?"

I shake my head no and drop three cubes of sugar into my coffee.

She cradles the soy with her other arm then puts out her hand. "We went to school together, two years ago. You're Clay, right?"

I put down the mug then slide my hand into hers. Her palm is warm and soft.

"We had one class together," she says, "but we didn't talk much."

She looks a little familiar. Maybe her hair's different.

"You wouldn't recognize me," she says. "I've changed a lot since high school." She rolls her heavily made-up eyes. "Thank God."

I place a wooden stirrer into my coffee and mix it. "Which class did we have?"

"Wood Shop."

I still don't remember her.

"The only thing I got out of that class were splinters," she says. "Oh, and I made a piano bench. Still no piano, but at least I've got the bench. Do you remember what you made?"

I stir my coffee. "A spice rack." The creamer mixes in and the coffee turns a light brown with some dark coffee grounds rising to the surface.

"I always thought you were the nicest guy," she says. "In school, everyone thought so. Kind of quiet, but that's okay. Back then, people thought I talked too much."

A customer clears his throat at the counter. We both glance at him, but he doesn't look away from the drink list.

She turns back to me and we shake hands again. "Well, maybe I'll see you around, when there's more time to talk." Then she walks back behind the counter.

That's me. Nice Guy Clay.

Would she still say that if she heard these tapes?

I head to the back of Monet's, toward the closed door that leads to the patio. Along the way, tables full of people stretch their legs or tilt back their chairs to form an obstacle course that begs me to spill my drink.

A drop of warm coffee spills onto my finger. I watch it slide across my knuckles and drip to the floor. I rub the toe of my shoe over the spot till it disappears. And I recall, earlier today, watching a slip of paper fall outside the shoe store.

After Hannah's suicide, but before the shoebox of tapes arrived, I found myself walking by Hannah's mom and dad's shoe store many times. It was that store that brought her to town in the first place. After thirty years in business, the owner of the store was looking to sell and retire. And Hannah's parents were looking to move.

I'm not sure why I walked by there so many times. Maybe I was searching for a connection to her, some connection outside of school, and it's the only one I could think of. Looking for answers to questions I didn't know how to ask. About her life. About everything.

I had no idea the tapes were on their way to explain it all.

The day after her suicide was the first time I found myself at their store, standing outside the front door. The lights were out. A single sheet of paper taped to the front window said, WELL BE OPEN SOON in thick black marker.

It was written in a hurry, I figured. They just forgot the apostrophe.

On the glass door, a delivery person had left a self-adhesive note. Among a list of other options, "Will try again tomorrow" was checked.

A few days later, I went back. Even more notes were stuck to the glass.

On my way home from school earlier today, I went by the store one more time. As I read the dates and notes on each piece of paper, the oldest note became unstuck and fluttered to the ground, resting beside my shoe. I picked it up and searched the door for the most recent note. Then I lifted a corner of that note and stuck the older one beneath it.

They'll be back soon, I thought. They must have taken her home for the burial. Back to her old town. Unlike old age or cancer, no one anticipates a suicide. They simply left without a chance to get things in order.

I open the patio door at Monet's, careful not to spill any more of my coffee.

Around the garden, to keep the atmosphere relaxed, the lights are kept low. Every table, including Hannah's in the far back corner, is occupied. Three guys in baseball caps sit there, hunched over textbooks and notebooks, none of them talking.

I go back inside and sit at a small table near a window. It overlooks the garden, but Hannah's table is hidden by a brick column choked with ivy.

I take a deep breath.

As the stories go by, one by one, I find myself relieved when my name isn't mentioned. Followed by a fear of what she hasn't yet said, of what she's going to say, when my turn comes.

Because my turn is coming. I know that. And I want it to be over with.

What did I do to you, Hannah?

▶

While I wait for her first words, I stare out the window. It's darker outside than in here. When I pull my gaze back and focus my eyes, I can see my own reflection in the glass.

And I look away.

I glance down at the Walkman on the table. There's still no sound, but the Play button is pressed. Maybe the tape didn't lock in place.

So I hit Stop.

■

Then Play again.

▶

Nothing.

I roll my thumb over the volume dial. The static in the headphones gets louder so I turn it back down. And I wait.

Shh! . . . if you're talking in the library.

Her voice, it's a whisper.

Shh! . . . in a movie theater or church.

I listen closer.

Sometimes there's no one around to tell you to be quiet . . . to be very, very quiet. Sometimes you need to be quiet when you're all alone. Like me, right now.

Shh!

At the crowded tables that fill the rest of the room, people talk. But the only words I understand are Hannah's. The other words become a muffled background noise occasionally tipped by a sharp laugh.

For example, you'd better be quiet—extremely quiet—if you're going to be a Peeping Tom. Because what if they heard?

I let out a breath of air. It's not me. Still not me.

What if she . . . what if I . . . found out?

Guess what, Tyler Down? I found out.

I lean back in my chair and close my eyes.

I feel sorry for you, Tyler. I do. Everyone else on these tapes, so far, must feel a little relieved. They came off as liars or jerks or insecure people lashing out at others. But your story, Tyler . . . it's kind of creepy.

I take my first sip of coffee.

A Peeping Tom? Tyler? I never knew.

And I feel a little creepy telling it, too. Why? Because I'm trying to get closer to you, Tyler. I'm trying to understand the excitement of staring through someone's bedroom window. Watching someone who doesn't know they're being watched. Trying to catch them in the act of . . .

What were you trying to catch me in the act of, Tyler? And were you disappointed? Or pleasantly surprised?

Okay, a show of hands, please. Who knows where I am?

I set down my coffee, lean forward, and try to imagine her recording this.

Where is she?

Who knows where I'm standing right now?

Then I get it and shake my head, feeling so embarrassed for him.

If you said, "Outside Tyler's window," you're right. And that's A-4 on your maps.

Tyler's not home right now . . . but his parents are. And

I really hope they don't come outside. Fortunately, there's a tall, thick bush just below his window, similar to my own window, so I'm feeling pretty safe.

How are you feeling, Tyler?

I can't imagine what it was like for him to mail out these tapes. To know he was sending his secret into the world.

There's a meeting of the yearbook staff tonight, which I know involves a lot of pizza and gossip. So I know you won't be home until after it gets all nice and dark. Which, as an amateur Peeping Tom, I appreciate very much.

So thank you, Tyler. Thanks for making this so easy.

When Tyler heard this, was he sitting here at Monet's, trying to look calm while sweating up a storm? Or was he lying in bed staring bug-eyed out his window?

Let's take a peek inside before you get home, shall we? The hallway light's on so I can see in pretty well. And yes, I see exactly what I expected—there's a bunch of camera equipment lying around.

You've got quite a collection here, Tyler. A lens for every occasion.

Including nightvision. Tyler won a statewide contest with that lens. Firstplace in the humor category. An old man walking his dog at night. The dog stopped to pee on a tree and Tyler snapped the picture. Nightvision made it look like a green laser beam blasting out of the dog's crotch.

I know, I know. I can hear you now. "Those are for the

yearbook, Hannah. I'm the student-life photographer." And I'm sure that's why your parents were fine spending that kind of cash. But is that the only way you use this stuff? Candid shots of the student body?

Ah, yes. Candid shots of the student body.

Before coming out here, I took the initiative to look up "candid" in the dictionary. It's one of those words with many definitions, but there's one that's most appropriate. And here it is, memorized for your pleasure: Relating to photography of subjects acting naturally or spontaneously without being posed.

So tell me, Tyler, those nights you stood outside my window, was I spontaneous enough for you? Did you catch me in all my natural, unposed . . .

Wait. Did you hear that?

I sit up and lean my elbows on the table.

A car coming up the road.

I cup my hands over both ears.

Is it you, Tyler? It sure is getting close. And there are the headlights.

I can hear it, just under Hannah's voice. The engine.

My heart definitely thinks it's you. My God, it's pounding.

The car's turning up the driveway.

Behind her voice, tires roll across pavement. The engine idles.

It's you, Tyler. It's you. You haven't stopped the engine so

I'm going to keep talking. And yes, this is exciting. I can definitely see the thrill.

It must have been terrifying for him to hear this. And it must be hell knowing he's not the only one.

Okay, listeners, ready? Car door . . . and . . .

Shh!

A long pause. Her breathing is soft. Controlled.

A door slams. Keys. Footsteps. Another door unlocks.

Okay, Tyler. Here's the play-by-play. You're inside the house with the door shut. You're either checking in with Mom and Dad, saying everything went great and this is going to be the best yearbook ever, or they didn't buy enough pizza and you're heading straight for the kitchen.

As we wait, I'm going to go back and tell everyone how this all began. And if I'm wrong with the timeline, Tyler, find the other people on these tapes and let them know that you started peeping way before I caught you.

You'll do that, right? All of you? You'll fill in the gaps? Because every story I'm telling leaves so many unanswered questions.

Unanswered? I would've answered any question, Hannah. But you never asked.

For example, how long were you stalking me, Tyler? How did you know my parents were out of town that week?

Instead of asking questions, that night at the party, you started yelling at me.

Okay, confession time. The rule around my house when the parents are away is that I'm not allowed to date. Their feeling, though they won't bring themselves to say it, is that I might enjoy the date too much and ask the boy to come inside.

In previous stories, I told you that the rumors you've all heard about me weren't true. And they're not. But I never claimed to be a Goody Two-Shoes. I did go out when my parents weren't home, but only because I could stay out as long as I wanted. And as you know, Tyler, on the night this all began, the boy I went out with walked me all the way to my front door. He stood there while I pulled out my keys to unlock the door . . . then he left.

I'm afraid to look, but I wonder if people in Monet's are staring at me. Can they tell, based on my reactions, that it's not music I'm listening to?

Or maybe no one's noticed. Why would they? Why should they care what I'm listening to?

Tyler's bedroom light is still off, so either he's having a detailed conversation with his parents or he's still hungry. Fine, have it your way, Tyler. I'll just keep talking about you.

Were you hoping I'd invite the guy in? Or would that have made you jealous?

I stir my coffee with the wooden stick.

Either way, after I went inside—alone!—I washed my

face and brushed my teeth. And the moment I stepped into my room . . . Click.

We all know the sound a camera makes when it snaps a picture. Even some of the digitals do it for nostalgia's sake. And I always keep my window open, about an inch or two, to let in fresh air. Which is how I knew someone was standing outside.

But I denied it. It was way too creepy to admit to myself on the very first night of my parents' vacation. I was only freaking myself out, I said. Just getting used to being alone.

Still, I wasn't dumb enough to change in front of the window. So I sat down on my bed. Click.

Such an idiot, Tyler. In middle school, some people thought you were mentally challenged. But you weren't. You were just an idiot.

Or maybe it wasn't a click, I told myself. Maybe it was a creak. My bed has a wooden frame that creaks a little. That was it. It had to be a creak.

I pulled the blankets over my body and undressed beneath them. Then I put on my pajamas, doing everything as slowly as possible, afraid whoever was outside might snap another picture. After all, I wasn't totally sure what a Peeping Tom got off on.

But wait—another picture would prove he was there, right? Then I could call the police and . . .

But the truth is, I didn't know what to hope for. My

parents weren't home. I was alone. I figured ignoring him was my best option. And even though he was outside, I was too afraid of what might happen if he saw me reaching for the phone.

Stupid? Yes. But did it make sense? Yes . . . at the time.

You should've called the cops, Hannah. It might have stopped this snowball from picking up speed. The one you keep talking about.

The one that ran over all of us.

So why was it so easy for Tyler to see into my room to begin with? Is that what you're asking? Do I always sleep with my shades wide open?

Good question, victim-blamers. But it wasn't that easy. The window blinds were kept at an angle exactly as I liked them. On clear nights, with my head on the pillow, I could fall asleep looking at the stars. And on stormy nights I could watch lightning light up the clouds.

I've done that, fallen asleep looking outside. But from the second floor, I don't need to worry about people seeing in.

When my dad found out I kept the blinds open—even a crack—he walked out to the sidewalk to make sure no one could see me from the street. And they couldn't. So he walked from the sidewalk, straight across the yard, up to my window. And what did he find? That unless they were pretty tall and standing right outside my window on their tiptoes, I was invisible.

So how long did you stand like that, Tyler? It must have been pretty uncomfortable. And if you were willing to go through all that trouble just to get a peek at me, I hope you got at least something out of it.

He did. But not what he wanted. Instead, he got this.

Had I known it was Tyler at the time, had I snuck under the blinds and looked up to see his face, I would've run outside and embarrassed the hell out of him.

In fact, that brings up the most interesting part of . . .

Wait! Here you come. We'll save that story for later.

I push my mug of coffee, not even half finished, to the far end of the table.

Let me describe Tyler's window for the rest of you. The shades are all the way down, yet I can see in. They're made of bamboo, or fake bamboo, and between each stick are varying amounts of space. If I stand on my tiptoes, like Tyler, I can reach a fairly wide-open gap and see in.

Okay, he's turning on the light and . . . he shuts the door. He's . . . he's sitting on the bed. He's yanking off his shoes and . . . now his socks.

I groan. Please don't do anything stupid, Tyler. It's your room, you can do what you want, but don't embarrass yourself anymore.

Maybe I should warn him. Give him a chance to hide. To undress underneath the covers. Maybe I should tap on the window. Or pound or kick on the wall. Maybe I should give him the same paranoia he gave me.

She's getting louder. Does she want to get caught?

After all, that's why I'm here, right? Revenge?

No. Revenge would have been fun. Revenge, in a twisted way, would have given me some sense of satisfaction. But this, standing outside Tyler's window, satisfies nothing. My mind is made up.

So why? Why am I here?

Well, what have I said? I just said I'm not here for me. And if you pass the tapes on, no one but those of you on the list will ever hear what I'm saying. So why am I here?

Tell us. Please, Hannah. Tell me why I'm listening to this. Why me?

I'm not here to watch you, Tyler. Calm down. I don't care what you're doing. In fact, I'm not even watching you right now. My back's against the wall and I'm staring at the street.

It's one of those streets with trees on either side, their branches meeting high above like fingertips touching. Sounds poetic, doesn't it? I even wrote a poem once comparing streets like this to my favorite childhood rhyme: Here is the church, here is the steeple, open it up . . . yadda, yadda, yadda.

One of you even read that poem I wrote. We'll talk about that later.

Again, it's not me. I didn't even know Hannah wrote poetry.

But I'm talking about Tyler now. And I'm still on Tyler's street. His dark and empty street. He just doesn't know I'm here . . . yet. So let's wrap this up before he goes to bed.

At school the next day, after Tyler's visit to my window, I told a girl who sat in front of me what happened. This girl's known for being a good listener, and sympathetic, and I wanted someone to be afraid for me. I wanted someone to validate my fears.

Well, she was definitely not the girl for that job. This girl's got a twisted side that very few of you know about.

"A Peeping Tom?" she said. "You mean, a real one?"

"I think so," I told her.

"I always wondered what that'd be like," she said. "Having a Peeping Tom is kind of . . . I don't know . . . sexy."

Definitely twisted. But who is she?

And why do I care?

She smiled and raised an eyebrow. "Do you think he'll come back?"

Honestly, the thought of him coming back never occurred to me. But now it was freaking me out. "What if he does?" I asked.

"Then you'll have to tell me about it," she said. And then she turned back around, ending our conversation.

Now, this girl and I had never hung out. We took a lot of the same electives, we were nice to each other in class, and sometimes we talked about hanging out, but we never did.

Here, I thought, was a golden opportunity.

I tapped her on the shoulder and told her that my parents were out of town. How would she like to come over and catch a Peeping Tom?

After school I went home with her to grab her stuff. Then she came over to my house. Since it was a weeknight and she was probably going to be out late, she told her parents we were working on a school project.

God. Does everyone use that excuse?

We finished our homework at the dining room table, waiting for it to get dark outside. Her car was parked out front as bait.

Two girls. Irresistible, right?

I squirm a little, shifting in my seat.

We moved into my bedroom and sat cross-legged on the bed, facing each other, talking about everything imaginable. To catch our Peeping Tom, we knew we needed to keep the talking quiet. We needed to hear that first . . . Click.

Her mouth dropped open. Her eyes, I've never seen them that happy.

She whispered for me to keep talking. "Pretend you didn't hear. Just play along."

I nodded.

Then she covered her mouth and ad-libbed. "Oh my God! You let him touch you where?"

We "gossiped" for a couple minutes, trying to hold back

any inappropriate laughter—the kind that would've given us away. But the clicking stopped and we were running out of things to gossip about.

"You know what I could use?" she asked. "A nice, deep, back massage."

"You're evil," I whispered.

She winked at me, then got up on her knees and worked her hands forward like a cat stretching until she was all the way down on my bed. Click.

I sincerely hope you burned or erased those pictures, Tyler. Because if they get out, even if it's not your fault, I'd hate to think what might happen to you.

I straddled her back. Click.

Pushed aside her hair. Click.

And began rubbing her shoulders. Click. Click.

She turned away from the window and whispered, "You know what it means if he stops taking pictures, right?"

I told her I didn't.

"It means he's doing something else." Click.

"Oh well," she said.

I kept rubbing her shoulders. In fact, I thought I was doing a pretty good job because she stopped talking and her lips curled into a beautiful smile. But then she whispered a new idea. A way to catch this pervert in the act.

I told her no. One of us should just leave the room, say we need to use the bathroom, and call the cops. We could end it right there.

But that didn't happen.

"No way," she said. "I'm not leaving until I find out if I know him. What if he goes to our school?"

"What if he does?" I asked.

She told me to follow her lead, then she rolled out from under my legs. According to her plan, when she said "three," I was to charge the window. But I thought the Peeping Tom might have left—might have gotten scared—because there hadn't been a click since I climbed off of her.

"It's time for some body lotion," she said. Click.

That sound sent my anger through the roof. Okay. I can play this game, I thought. "Look in my top drawer."

She pointed to the drawer nearest the window and I nodded.

Beneath my arms, my shirt is slightly damp. I shift uncomfortably in my seat again. But, God, I can't stop listening.

She pulled open the drawer, looked inside, and covered her mouth.

What? There was nothing in my drawer worthy of a reaction like that. There was nothing in my whole room worthy of that.

"I didn't know you were into this," she said, nice and loud. "We should use it . . . together."

"Um, okay," I said.

She reached into the drawer, pushed some things

around, then covered her mouth again. "Hannah?" she said. "How many of these do you have? You are definitely a naughty girl." Click. Click.

Very clever, I thought. "Why don't you count them?"

So she did. "Let's see, now. Here's one . . . and two . . . "

I slid one foot off the bed.

" . . . three!"

I jumped at the window and yanked the cord. The blinds flew up. I looked for your face but you were moving so fast.

The other girl, she wasn't looking at your face, Tyler.

"Oh my God!" she screamed. "He's cramming his dick in his pants."

Tyler, wherever you are, I am so sorry. You deserve this, but I'm sorry.

So who were you? I saw your height and your hair, but I couldn't see your face clearly enough.

Still, you gave yourself up, Tyler. The next day at school I asked so many people the exact same question, Where were you last night? Some said they were at home or at a friend's house. Or at the movies. None of your business. But you, Tyler, you had the most defensive—and interesting—response of all.

"What, me? Nowhere."

And for some reason, telling me you were nowhere made your eyes twitch and your forehead break into a sweat.

You are such an idiot, Tyler.

Hey, at least you're original. And at least you stopped

coming around my house. But your presence, Tyler, that never left.

After your visits, I twisted my blinds shut every night. I locked out the stars and I never saw lightning again. Each night, I simply turned out the lights and went to bed.

Why didn't you leave me alone, Tyler? My house. My bedroom. They were supposed to be safe for me. Safe from everything outside. But you were the one who took that away.

Well . . . not all of it.

Her voice trembles.

But you took away what was left.

She pauses. And within that silence I realize how intensely I've been staring at nothing. Staring in the direction of my mug on the far end of the table. But not at it.

I want to, but I'm too intimidated to look at the people around me. They have to be watching me now. Trying to understand the pained look on my face. Trying to figure out who this poor kid is, listening to outdated audiotapes.

So how important is your security, Tyler? What about your privacy? Maybe it's not as important to you as it was for me, but that's not for you to decide.

I look through the window, past my reflection, to the barely lit patio garden. I can't tell if anyone's still there, beyond the brick-and-ivy column, sitting at her table.

A table that, at one time, was Hannah's other safe place.

So who was this mystery girl featured in your story, Tyler? Who smiled so beautifully when I rubbed her back?

Who helped me expose you? Should I tell?

That depends. What did she ever do to me?

For the answer . . . insert tape three.

But I'm ready for it to be me, Hannah. I'm ready to get this over with.

Oh, and Tyler, I'm standing outside your window again. I walked away to finish your story, but your bedroom light has been out for some time . . . so I'm back now.

There's a long pause. A rustling of leaves.

Knock-knock, Tyler.

I hear it. She taps on the window. Twice.

Don't worry. You'll find out soon enough.

■

I slip off the headphones, wrap the yellow cord tightly around the Walkman, and tuck it in my jacket pocket.

Across the room, Monet's bookshelf is loaded with old books. Discards, mostly. Paperback westerns, New Age, sci-fi.

Carefully weaving through the crowded tables, I walk over to it.

A massive thesaurus sits beside a dictionary that's missing its hardcover spine. Down the exposed paper spine someone wrote DICTIONARY in heavy black ink. Stacked on the same shelf, each in a different color, are five books. They're approximately the same size as yearbooks, but purchased for their blank pages. Scribble books, they call them. Each year, a new one is added and people scrawl whatever they want inside. They mark special occasions, write horrible poetry, sketch things that are beautiful or grotesque, or just rant.

Each book has a scrap of duct tape on the spine with a year written on it. I pull out the one from our freshman year. With all the time Hannah spent at Monet's, maybe she wrote something in here. Like a poem. Or maybe she had other talents I didn't know about. Maybe she knew how to draw. I'm just looking for something apart from the ugliness of these tapes. I need that right now. I need to see her in a different way.

Since most people date their entries, I flip toward the back. To September. And there it is.

To keep the page, I shut the book on my index finger and take it back to my table. I take a slow sip of lukewarm coffee, reopen the book, and read the words scribbled in red ink near the top: Everyone needs an olly-olly-oxen-free.

It's signed with three sets of initials: J.D. A.S. H.B.

Jessica Davis. Alex Standall. Hannah Baker.

Below the initials, pressed into the crease between the pages, someone stuck an upside-down photograph. I pull it out, flip it over, then spin it rightside up.

It's Hannah.

God, I love her smile. And her hair, it's still long. One of her arms is wrapped around the waist of another student.

Courtney Crimsen. And behind them is a crowd of students. Everyone's either holding a bottle, a can, or a red plastic cup. It's dark at the party and Courtney doesn't look happy. But she doesn't look mad, either.

She looks nervous, I think.

Why?

CASSETTE 3: SIDE A

▶

Courtney Crimsen. What a pretty name. And yes, a very pretty girl, as well. Pretty hair. Pretty smile. Perfect skin.

And you're also very nice. Everyone says so.

I stare at the picture in the scribble book. Hannah's arm around Courtney's waist at some random party. Hannah is happy. Courtney is nervous. But I have no idea why.

Yes, Courtney, you're sweet to everyone you meet in the halls. You're sweet to everyone as they walk with you to your car after school.

I sip my coffee, which is getting cold.

You're definitely one of the most popular girls in school. And you . . . are . . . just . . . so . . . sweet. Right?

Wrong.

I pound back the coffee to empty the mug.

Yes, my dear listeners, Courtney is nice to whomever she comes in contact with or whomever she's talking to. And yet, ask yourselves—is it all a show?

I carry my mug to the pour-it-yourself bar for a refill.

I think it is. Now, let me tell you why.

First off, to everyone listening, I doubt Tyler will let you see the pictures he took of me giving Courtney a backrub.

The container of half-n-half slips from my grip and clatters to the counter. I catch it before it falls to the floor, then look over my shoulder. The girl behind the register tips her head back and laughs.

Courtney's the one from Hannah's room?

Hannah takes an extra-long pause. She knows that info needs to sink in.

If you have seen those pictures, lucky you. I'm sure they're very sexy. But as you now know, they're also very posed.

Posed. What an interesting word to sum up Courtney's tale. Because when you're posed, you know someone's watching. You put on your very best smile. You let your sweetest personality shine.

Unlike Courtney's photo in the scribble book.

And in high school, people are always watching so there's always a reason to pose.

I press the top of the urn and a stream of dark coffee spills into the mug.

I don't think you do this intentionally, Courtney. And

that's why I put you on these tapes. To let you know that what you do affects others. More specifically, it affected me.

Courtney does come off as genuinely sweet. Hearing her story here, on these tapes, must have killed her.

A shiver crawls up my back. "Killed her." A phrase I will now drop from my vocabulary.

Courtney Crimsen. The name sounds almost too perfect. And as I said, you look perfect, too. The only thing left . . . is to be perfect.

With my coffee, cream, and sugar cubes mixed, I return to my table.

So that's where I give you credit. You could have taken the bitch route and still had all the friends and boyfriends you could handle. But instead you took the sweet route, so everyone would like you and not a soul would hate you.

Let me be very clear. I do not hate you, Courtney. In fact, I don't even dislike you. But for a time, I thought you and I were becoming friends.

I don't remember that. I don't think I ever saw them hanging out.

It turns out you were just grooming me to be another tally mark under People Who Think Courtney Crimsen Is a Really Neat Girl. Another guaranteed vote for Most Liked in the senior yearbook.

And once you did it to me, and I realized it, I watched you do it to others.

Here, Courtney, is your contribution to the anthology of my life.

Did you like that? The anthology of my life?

I just made it up.

I pull my backpack onto my lap and unzip the largest pocket.

The day after Tyler took the candid shots of our student bodies began like any other. The bell to first period rang and Courtney, as usual, ran in a couple seconds late. Not that it mattered, because Mrs. Dillard wasn't there yet, either.

Also not unusual.

I remove Hannah's map and unfold it on the small table.

When you were done chatting to the person in front of you, Courtney, I tapped you on the shoulder. The moment you looked into my eyes, we both began laughing. We spoke a bunch of two- or three-word sentences but I don't remember who said what, because whatever you said were my thoughts, as well.

"So weird."

"I know."

"What the hell?"

"Can you imagine?"

"So funny."

Then, when Mrs. Dillard finally came in, you turned around to face the front of the room. And when class was over, you left.

I search the map for the red star at Tyler's house. Part of me feels strange about keeping such a close track of Hannah's story. Like I'm obsessed. Too obsessed. While another part of me wants to deny the obsession.

It wasn't until I stepped into the hall on my way to second period that I thought, Wait a sec. She didn't say good-bye.

I'm just doing what she asked. That's not obsession. It's respect. I'm living out her last requests.

Did you say good-bye on any other day? No, not often. But after the previous night, this time it felt intentional. I guess I thought that after what we'd experienced less than twenty-four hours before, we would now be more than just casual acquaintances.

A-4. A red star on Tyler's house.

But that, evidently, is what we'd become once again. We said hello in the halls and sometimes you said good-bye to me after class, but never more than you said it to anyone else.

Until the night of the party.

Until the night you needed me again.

II

I need a moment to catch up. I can't listen anymore till I do that.

I slip off the headphones and hang them around my neck. The girl I took Wood Shop with walks around with a plastic tub, gathering mugs and plates from empty tables. I look away toward the dark window when she clears the place next to me. Her reflection glances my way several times, but I don't turn around.

When she leaves, I sip my coffee and try my hardest not to think. I just wait.

Fifteen minutes later, a bus drives by the front door of Monet's and the waiting is over. I grab the map, toss my backpack over my shoulder, and run out the door.

The bus is stopped at the far corner. I race down the sidewalk, up the bus steps, and find an empty seat near the middle.

The driver looks at me in the rearview mirror. "I'm ahead of schedule," he says. "We'll be sitting here a couple minutes."

I nod, press the headphones into my ears, and look out the window.

▶

Let me tell you that there is a much bigger, more important party later in the tapes.

Is that it? Is that where I come in?

But this is the party that brings Courtney into the mix.

I was at school, backpack on my shoulder, heading out of first period when you grabbed my hand.

"Hannah, wait up," you said. "How are you?"

Your smile, your teeth . . . flawless.

I probably said, "Fine," or, "Good. How are you?" But truthfully, I didn't care, Courtney. Every time our eyes caught each other in a crowded hall and I watched your gaze jump to someone else, I lost a little more respect for you. And sometimes I wondered how many people in that one hallway felt the same.

You went on to ask if I'd heard about the party later that night. I said that I had, but that I didn't feel like going and wandering around looking for someone to talk to. Or I didn't feel like wandering around looking for someone to save me from talking to someone else.

"We should go together," you said. And you tilted your head to the side, flashed your smile, and—though I'm probably imagining this—I think I even saw you bat your eyes.

Yeah, that's Courtney. No one can resist her, and she flirts with everyone.

"Why?" I asked. "Why should we go to a party together?"

That obviously took you by surprise. I mean, you are who you are and everyone wants to go to a party with you. To at least be seen entering a party with you. Everyone! Boys. Girls. It doesn't matter. That's the kind of admiration people have for you.

Have? Or had? Because I have a feeling that's about to change.

Most of them, unfortunately, don't realize how carefully you plan that image.

You repeated my question. "Why should we go to a party together? Hannah, so we can hang out."

I asked why you wanted to hang out after ignoring me for so long. But of course, you denied ignoring me at all. You said I must have misread things. And the party would be a good chance to get to know each other better.

And although I was still suspicious, you are who you are and everyone wants to go to a party with you.

But you knew, Hannah. You knew, but you still went. Why?

"Great!" you said. "Can you drive?"

And my heart tumbled a bit.

But I pulled it back up and ignored my suspicions once again. "Sure, Courtney," I said. "What time?"

You flipped open your notebook and ripped out a piece of paper. In tiny blue letters you wrote your address, the time, and your initials: C.C. You handed me the paper, said, "This is going to be great!" then gathered up your stuff and left.

The bus door slides shut and we pull away from the curb.

Guess what, Courtney? On your way out the door, you forgot to say good-bye.

So here's my theory as to why you wanted to go to a party with me: You knew I was pissed at being ignored by you. At the very least, you knew I was hurt. And that was not good for your flawless reputation. That had to be fixed.

D-4 on your map, everybody. Courtney's house.

I reopen the map.

When I pulled up to the curb, your front door flew open. Out you came, bounding off the porch and down the walkway. Your mom, before shutting the front door, bent down to get a good look inside my car.

Don't worry, Mrs. Crimsen, I thought. No boys in here. No alcohol. No drugs. No fun.

Why do I feel so compelled to follow her map? I don't need to. I'm listening to the tapes, every single one, front and back, and that should be enough.

But it's not.

You opened the passenger door, sat down, and buckled up. "Thanks for the lift," you said.

I'm not following the map because she wants me to. I'm following it because I need to understand. Whatever it takes, I need to truly understand what happened to her.

A lift? Already having doubts about why you invited me, that was not the hello I wanted to hear.

D-4. It's only a handful of blocks from Tyler's house.

I wanted to be wrong about you, Courtney. I did. I wanted you to see it as me picking you up so we could go to a party together. And that is very different from me giving you a lift.

At that moment, I knew how the party would play out for us. But how it ended? Well, that was a surprise. That . . . was weird.

Bolted to the back of each seat, behind a square sheet of Plexiglas, is a map of all the city's bus routes. From where I caught this one, the bus will drive by Courtney's house, turn left a block before Tyler's, then stop.

We parked two and a half blocks away, which was actually the closest spot we could get. I have one of those car stereos that continues playing even after I shut off the engine. It won't stop until someone opens a door. But that night, when I opened the door, the music didn't stop . . . it just sounded distant.

"Oh my God," you said. "I think that music's coming from the party!"

Did I mention we were two and a half blocks away? That's how loud it was. That party was absolutely begging for a police visit.

Which is why I don't go to many parties. I'm so close to being valedictorian. One mistake could mess it all up for me.

We took our place in the stream of students heading to the party—like joining a bunch of salmon heading upstream to mate. When we got there, two football players—never to be seen at a party without their jerseys—stood on opposite sides of the gate collecting beer money. So I reached into my pocket for some cash.

Over the loud music, you shouted to me, "Don't worry about it."

We got to the gate and one of they guys said, "Two bucks a cup." Then he realized who he was talking to. "Oh. Hey, Courtney. Here you go." And he handed you a red plastic cup.

Two bucks? That's it? They must charge girls differently.

You nodded your head in my direction. The guy smiled, then handed me a cup. But when I grabbed for it, he didn't let go. He told me his replacement was coming any minute and that we should hang out. I smiled at him, but you grabbed me by the arm and pulled me through the gate.

"Don't," you said. "Trust me."

I asked why, but you were scanning the crowd and didn't hear me.

I don't remember any stories of Courtney and any football players. Basketball players, yes. Many of them. But football? None.

Then you said we should split up. And do you want to know my first thought when you said that, Courtney? Gee, that sure didn't take long.

You said there were a few people you needed to see and that we should meet up later. I lied and said there were some people I needed to see, too.

Then you told me not to leave without you. "You're my ride, remember?"

How could I forget, Courtney?

The bus turns onto Courtney's street, with For Sale signs posted in about a third of the yards. When we pass

Courtney's house, I half expect to see a red star spray-painted on the front door. But the porch is buried in darkness. No porch light. No lights in any window at all.

But you smiled at me. And finally, you said the magic word. "Good-bye." And good-bye was exactly what you meant.

"Miss your stop, Clay?"

An icy chill shoots up my spine.

A voice. A girl's voice. But not from the headphones.

II

Someone called my name. But from where?

Across the aisle, the dark belt of windows acts like a mirror. I see the reflection of a girl sitting behind me. Maybe my age. But do I know her? I turn my body around and look over the backrest.

Skye Miller. My eighth-grade crush. She smiles, or maybe it's more of a smirk, because she knows she startled the hell out of me.

Skye's always been pretty, but she acts like the thought's never crossed her mind. Especially the past couple of years. She dresses in dull, loose clothing every day. Almost burying herself within them. Tonight, it's a bulky gray sweatshirt and matching pants.

I pull the headphones from my ears. "Hey, Skye."

"Miss your house?" she asks. More words than she's spoken

to me in a long time. More words than I've heard her speak to anyone in a long time. "He'll stop if you ask him to."

I shake my head. No. Not my house.

The bus takes a left at the next intersection and pulls up to the curb. The door slides open and the driver yells back, "Anyone?"

I look to the front of the bus, into the rearview mirror, and catch the driver's eye. Then I turn back to Skye. "Where are you going?" I ask.

The smirk returns. Her eyes stay focused on mine. She's trying so hard to make me feel uncomfortable. And it's working.

"I'm not going anywhere," she finally says.

Why does she do this? What happened between eighth grade and now? Why does she insist on being an outcast? What changed? No one knows. One day, at least it seemed that fast, she just stopped wanting to be a part of anything.

But this is my stop and I should get off. It's halfway between two of the red stars: Tyler's house and Courtney's.

Or instead, I could stay and talk with Skye. To be more exact, I could stay and *try* to talk with her. An almost guaranteed one-way conversation.

"See you tomorrow," she says.

And that's it. The conversation's over. Part of me, I admit, is relieved.

"See you later," I say.

I lift my backpack over my shoulder and walk to the front of the bus. I thank the driver and return to the cold air outside. The door shuts behind me. The bus pulls away. Skye's window passes with her head resting against the glass and her eyes shut.

I pull my backpack onto both shoulders and tighten the straps. Alone once again, I start walking. To Tyler's house.

Okay, but how will I know which one it is? This is the block, I know that, and it's this side of the block, but Hannah gave no address.

If his bedroom light's on, maybe I'll see the bamboo shutters.

With each house I walk by, trying not to stare too long, I look for those shutters.

Maybe I'll get lucky. Maybe there will be a sign posted in his yard. PEEPING TOM—COME INSIDE.

I can't stifle a laugh at my own lame joke.

With Hannah's words ready at the push of a button, it feels wrong to smile like this. But it also feels nice. It feels like the first time I've smiled in months, though it's only been hours.

Then, two houses away, I see it.

I stop smiling.

The bedroom light is on and the bamboo shutters are down. A spiderweb of silver duct tape holds the fractured window together.

Was it a rock? Did someone throw a rock at Tyler's window?

Was it someone who knew? Someone from the list?

As I get closer I can almost picture her, Hannah, standing beside his window whispering into a recorder. Words too soft for me to hear at this distance. But in the end, the words reach me.

A square hedge divides Tyler's front yard from the next. I walk toward it to shield myself from view. Because he has to be watching. Looking out. Waiting for someone to bust his window wide open.

"You want to throw something?"

The icy chill comes slicing back. I spin around, ready to hit someone and run.

"Hold it! It's me."

Marcus Cooley, from school.

I lean forward, resting my hands on my knees. Exhausted. "What are you doing here?" I ask.

Marcus holds a fist-sized rock just below my eyes. "Take it," he says.

I look up at him. "Why?"

"You'll feel better, Clay. Honest."

I look over at the window. At the duct tape. Then I look down and close my eyes, shaking my head. "Let me guess, Marcus. You're on the tapes."

He doesn't answer. He doesn't need to. When I look up,

the corners of his eyes struggle to hold back a smile. And in that struggle, I can tell he's not ashamed.

I nod to Tyler's window. "Did you do that?"

He pushes the rock into my hand. "You'd be the first to say no, Clay."

My heart starts racing. Not from Marcus standing here, or Tyler standing somewhere inside, or the heavy rock in my hand, but from what he just told me.

"You're the third to come out here," he says. "Plus me."

I try to picture anyone other than Marcus, someone else on the list, throwing a rock at Tyler's window. But I can't. It doesn't make sense.

We're all on the list. All of us. We're all guilty of something. Why is Tyler any different than the rest of us?

I stare down at the rock in my hand. "Why are you doing this?" I ask.

He nods over his shoulder, down the block. "That's my house down there. With the light on. I've been watching Tyler's house to see who comes around."

I can't imagine what Tyler told his parents. Did he plead with them not to replace the window because more might be coming? And what did they say? Did they ask how he knew? Did they ask why?

"The first was Alex," Marcus says. He doesn't sound the least bit ashamed to be telling me this. "We were hanging out at my house when, out of nowhere, he wanted me to point out Tyler's house. I didn't know why, it's not like they were friends, but he really wanted to know."

"So, what, you just gave him a rock to throw at his window?"

"No. It was his idea. I didn't even know the tapes existed yet."

I toss the rock up a few inches then catch its weight in my other hand. Even before the previous rocks weakened it, the window would stand no chance against this. So why did Marcus choose this rock for me? He's heard the rest of the tapes, but he wants me to be the one to finish off the window. Why?

I toss the rock back to my other hand. Beyond his shoulder I can see the porch light at Marcus's house. I should make him tell me which window is his. I should tell him this rock is going through one of his house's windows, and he might as well tell me which one is his so I don't scare the hell out of his little sister.

I grip the rock hard. Harder. But there's no way to keep my voice from shaking. "You're a dick, Marcus."

"What?"

"You're on the tapes, too," I say. "Right?"

"So are you, Clay."

My voice shakes from both rage and an attempt to hold back tears. "What makes us so different from him?"

"He's a Peeping Tom," Marcus says. "He's a freak. He

looked in Hannah's window, so why not break his?"

"And you?" I ask. "What did you do?"

For a moment, his eyes stare through me. Then he blinks.

"Nothing. It's ridiculous," he says. "I don't belong on those tapes. Hannah just wanted an excuse to kill herself."

I let the rock drop onto the sidewalk. It was either that or smash it in his face right there.

"Get the hell away from me," I tell him.

"It's my street, Clay."

My fingers close and tighten into a fist. I look down at the rock, aching to pick it back up.

But I turn away. Fast. I walk the full length of the sidewalk in front of Tyler's house without looking at the window. I can't let myself think. I pull the headphones from my neck and place them back in my ears. I reach into my pocket and hit Play.

▶

Was I disappointed when you said good-bye to me, Courtney?

Not much. It's hard to be disappointed when what you expected turns out to be true.

Keep walking, Clay.

But did I feel used? Absolutely.

And yet the whole time Courtney was using me, she

probably thought she was polishing up her image in my eyes. Can you say . . . backfire?

That party turned into a night of firsts for me. I saw my very first fistfight—which was horrible. I have no idea what it was about, but it started right behind me. Two guys were shouting, and when I turned around, their chests were about an inch apart. A crowd began to form, egging them on. The mob became a thick wall, not about to let the situation die down. All they needed was for one chest to close the gap, even accidentally, and it was on.

And that's what happened.

The bump of a chest turned into a shove, which, right away, became a fist pounding a jaw.

After two more punches, I turned away and pushed through the wall of people, which, by that time, was four bodies deep. Some in the back were standing on tiptoes for a better view.

Disgusting.

I ran inside, searching for a bathroom to hide in. I didn't feel physically sick. But mentally . . . my mind was twisting in so many ways. The only thing I could think of was that I needed to vomit.

I pull out my map and look for the nearest star that isn't Courtney's. I'm not going there. I'm not listening to Hannah talk about her while I stare at her dark, empty house.

I'm on to the next thing.

In Health, we once saw a documentary on migraines. One of the men interviewed used to fall on his knees and bang his head against the floor, over and over during attacks. This diverted the pain from deep inside his brain, where he couldn't reach it, to a pain outside that he had control over. And in a way, by vomiting, that's what I hoped to do.

The exact locations of the red stars are hard to see if I don't stop walking, if I don't stand still beneath a streetlamp. But I can't stop walking. Not even for a moment.

Watching those guys pummel each other so no one would suspect them of being weak was too much for me. Their reputations were more important than their faces. And Courtney's reputation was more important than my reputation.

Did anyone at that party actually believe she brought me there as a friend? Or did they simply think I was her latest charity case?

I guess I'll never know.

I refold the map and tuck it under my arm.

Unfortunately, the only bathroom I found was occupied . . . so I went back outside. The fistfight was over, everything had returned to normal, and I needed to leave.

The temperature continues to fall and I tighten my arms around my chest as I walk.

When I approached the gate, the same gate where I entered the party, guess who was standing there all by himself.

Tyler Down . . . fully equipped with his camera.

It's time to leave Tyler alone, Hannah.

When he saw me, the look on his face was priceless. And pitiful. He crossed his arms, trying to shield the camera from my view. But why would he do that? Everyone knows he's on the yearbook staff.

But I asked anyway. "What's that for, Tyler?"

"What? Oh . . . this? Um . . . yearbook."

And then, from behind me, someone called my name. I'm not going to tell you who because it doesn't matter. Like the person who grabbed my ass at Blue Spot Liquor, what he was about to say was just an aftereffect of someone else's actions—someone else's callousness.

"Courtney said I should talk to you," he said.

I exhale quickly. After this, your reputation is ruined, Courtney.

I looked behind him. At the far end of the yard, three silver kegs sat in the middle of an inflatable pool full of ice. Beside the pool, Courtney was talking to three boys from another school.

The boy standing in front of me took a slow sip from his beer. "She says you're fun to hang out with."

And I started to soften. I started letting my guard down. Sure, maybe I was right and Courtney was only concerned with saving her image. Maybe she thought that by sending a cute boy over to talk to me I'd forget all about her ignoring me at the party.

Yes, he was kind of cute. And okay, maybe I was willing to have a little selective amnesia.

But something happened, Hannah. What?

After we spoke for a while, this guy said he had a confession to make. Courtney didn't actually send him over to talk to me. But he did overhear her talking about me and that's why he came and found me.

I asked him what Courtney said, and he just smiled and looked down at the grass.

I was through with these games! I demanded to know what she said about me.

"That you're fun to hang out with," he repeated.

I started rebuilding my guard, brick by brick. "Fun . . . how?"

He shrugged.

"How?"

Ready for this, everyone? Our sweet little Miss Crimsen told this guy, and whoever else was standing within earshot, that I've got a few surprises buried in my dresser drawers.

My breath stops like I've been sucker punched in the stomach.

She made that up! Courtney completely made that up.

And out of the corner of my eye, I watched Tyler Down start walking away.

By now, the tears were welling up. "Did she say what was in there?" I asked.

Again, he smiled.

My face felt so hot, my hands started shaking, and I asked him why he believed her. "Do you believe everything people say about me?"

He told me to calm down, that it didn't matter.

"Yes!" I told him. "It does matter."

I left him to have a little conversation over by the keg pool. But on my way there, I had a better idea. I ran up to Tyler and stood in front of him. "You want a picture?" I said. "Follow me." Then I grabbed his arm and led him across the yard.

The picture! The one from the scribble book.

Tyler protested the whole way, thinking I wanted him to take a picture of the keg pool. "They'll never print it," he said. "You know, underage drinking?"

Right. Why would they want a yearbook that showed actual student life?

"Not that," I said. "I want you to take a picture of me. Me and Courtney."

I swear, at that moment his forehead was glistening. Me and the backrub girl, together again.

I asked if he was all right.

"Yeah, no, sure, fine." And that's an exact quote.

In the picture, Hannah's arm is wrapped around Courtney's waist. Hannah's laughing, but Courtney isn't. She's nervous.

And now I know why.

Courtney was in the middle of having her cup filled, and I told Tyler to wait right there. When Courtney saw me, she asked if I was having fun.

"Someone wants to take your picture," I said. Then I grabbed her by the arm and pulled her over to Tyler. I told her to put down her cup or the yearbook wouldn't be able to use it.

Tyler put it in the scribble book at Monet's. He wanted us to see it.

This was not a part of her plan. She only invited me to the party to clear her beautiful name after ignoring me for so long. A permanent photograph linking us to one another was not supposed to happen.

Courtney tried to pull out of my grip. "I . . . I don't want to," she said.

I whirled around to face her. "Why not, Courtney? Why did you invite me here? Please don't tell me I was just a chauffeur. I mean, I thought we were becoming friends."

He must have put it in the scribble book because he knew we would never find it in the yearbook. He would never turn it in. Not after learning what the photograph really meant.

"We are friends," she said.

"Then put down your drink," I said. "It's time for a picture."

Tyler aimed the camera and focused his lens, waiting for

our beautiful, natural smiles. Courtney lowered the drink to her side. I put my arm around her waist and told her, "If you ever want to borrow anything from my dresser, Courtney, all you need to do is ask."

"Ready?" Tyler said.

I leaned forward, pretending someone had just told me the funniest joke in the world. Click.

Then I told them I was leaving because the party sucked.

Courtney begged me to stay. She told me to be reasonable. And maybe I was being a little insensitive. I mean, she wasn't ready to leave. How would she get home if her chauffeur didn't wait around for her?

"Find another ride," I said. And I left.

Part of me wanted to cry for being so right about her invitation. Instead, on the long walk back to my car, I started laughing. And I shouted into the trees, "What is going on?"

And then someone called my name.

"What do you want, Tyler?"

He told me I was right about the party. "The party does suck."

"No, Tyler. It doesn't," I said. Then I asked why he was following me.

His eyes dropped to his camera and he fiddled with the lens. He needed a ride home, he said.

At that, I really started laughing. Not specifically at

what he said, but at the absurdity of the whole night. Did he really have no clue that I knew about his night prowling—about his nocturnal missions? Or did he sincerely hope I didn't know? Because as long as I didn't know, we could be friends, right?

"Fine," I said. "But we're not stopping anywhere."

A few times on the ride home he tried talking to me. But each time I cut him off. I did not want to act like everything was okay, because it wasn't.

And after I dropped him off, I took the longest possible route home.

I have a feeling I'll be doing the same.

I explored alleys and hidden roads I never knew existed. I discovered neighborhoods entirely new to me. And finally . . . I discovered I was sick of this town and everything in it.

I'm starting to get there, too, Hannah.

Next side.

■

CASSETTE 3: SIDE B

▶

How many of you remember the Oh My Dollar Valentines?

How many of us would rather forget?

Those were fun, weren't they? You fill out a survey, a computer analyzes your answers, then it cross-references with the other surveys. For just a buck, you get the name and number of your one true soul mate. For five bucks, you get your top five. And hey! All proceeds go to a worthy cause.

Cheer Camp.

Cheer Camp.

Each morning over the loudspeaker came the cheery announcements. "Don't forget, there's only four more days to turn in your surveys. Only four more lonely days until your true love is revealed."

And every morning, a new peppy cheerleader continued the countdown. "Only three more days. . . . Only two more days. . . . Just one more day. . . . Today's the day!"

For every foot of sidewalk I put between Tyler's house, Marcus, and me, the muscles in my shoulders relax a little more.

Then the whole squad of cheerleaders sang, "Oh my dollar, Oh my dollar, Oh my dol-lar Valentine!"

This, of course, was followed by whoops and hollers and cheers. I always imagined them doing kicks and splits and tossing their pom-poms around the attendance office.

I walked by the attendance office once, on an errand for a teacher, and that's exactly what they were doing.

And yes, I did fill out my survey. I've been a sucker for surveys my whole life. If you ever caught me reading one of those teen magazines, I swear, it wasn't for the makeup tips. It was for the surveys.

Because you never wore makeup, Hannah. You didn't need it.

Fine, some of the hair and makeup tips were helpful.

You wore makeup?

But I only picked the magazines up for the surveys. The tips were a bonus.

Do you remember those career surveys we had to fill out freshman year, the ones that were supposed to help us choose electives? According to my survey, I'd make a won-

derful lumberjack. And if that career didn't work out, I could use my fallback career as an astronaut.

An astronaut or a lumberjack? Seriously? Thanks for the help.

I don't remember my fallback career, but I got the lumberjack, too. I tried figuring out why the test saw that as my best career path. True, I marked down that I liked the outdoors, but who doesn't? It doesn't mean I like cutting down trees.

The Valentine survey was a two-parter. First, you described yourself. Hair color. Eye color. Height. Body type. Favorite type of music and movie. Then you put a check beside your top three things to do on weekends. Which is funny, because whoever designed the list forgot to mention drinking and sex—which would've been the most accurate response for most of our student body.

In all, there were about twenty questions. And I know, based on who appeared on my list, that not everyone answered honestly.

In the middle of the sidewalk, beneath a streetlamp, is a dark green metal bench. At one time, maybe this was a bus stop. But now, it's just a bench to relax on. For old people, or anyone, too tired to walk.

For me.

For part two of the survey, it was your turn to describe what you were looking for in a soul mate. Their height. Their body type. If they're athletic or not. Shy or outgoing.

I sit on the cold metal and lean forward, dropping my head into my hands. Only a handful of blocks from home, and I don't know where to go.

As I filled mine out, I found myself describing a certain someone at our school.

I should've answered my survey seriously.

You'd think that if my answers all described one person, that person would've at least appeared in my top five. But that person must have been immune to the cheerleaders and their cheers because he didn't end up on my list anywhere.

And no, I'm not telling you his name . . . yet.

For fun, I filled mine out as Holden Caulfield from *The Catcher in the Rye*, that semester's required reading and the first person to come to mind.

Holden. What a horrible first date that depressed loner would make.

The moment the surveys were distributed, in third-period history, I bubbled in my answers.

There sure were some weird names on my list. Exactly the sort of people I'd expect to fall for a Holden Caulfield.

It was your typical day in Coach Patrick's history class. Decipher a bunch of notes scribbled on the board probably five minutes before class started, then copy them down in your notebook. If you finish before the end of class, read pages eight through one ninety-four in your textbook . . . and don't fall asleep.

And no talking.

How was I to know every single one of those girls would call me? I assumed everyone at school saw the survey as a joke. Just a fund-raiser for Cheer Camp.

After class, I walked straight to the student body office. At the end of the counter, closest to the door, was the drop-off box—a large shoebox with a slit cut in the top and decorated with cutout pink and red hearts. The red hearts had OH MY DOLLAR VALENTINE! written on them. The pink ones had green dollar signs.

I folded my survey in half, slipped it into the box, then turned around to leave. But Ms. Benson, smiley as usual, was standing right there.

"Hannah Baker?" she said. "I didn't know you and Courtney Crimsen were friends."

The look on my face must have expressed exactly what I was thinking, because right away, she backpedaled. "At least, that's what I figured. That's what it looked like. I mean, you are friends, aren't you?"

That lady is beyond nosy.

My first thought was of Tyler standing outside my window . . . and I was furious! Was he actually showing off those Peeping Tom photos? To Ms. Benson?

No. Ms. Benson told me she had delivered some checks to the yearbook room that morning. Taped to the walls were sample shots that might appear in the yearbook. One particular photo was of Courtney and me.

You guessed it. The one from the party, with my arm

around her waist, looking like I was having the time of my life.

Quite an actress, Hannah.

I told her, "No, we're just acquaintances."

"Well, it's a really fun picture," Ms. Benson said. And this, these next words, I remember exactly: "The wonderful thing about a yearbook photo is that everyone shares the moment with you . . . forever."

It sounded like something she'd said a million times before. And before, I probably would have agreed. But not with that photo. Anyone looking at that photo would definitely not be sharing our moment. They could not come close to imagining my thoughts in that picture. Or Courtney's. Or Tyler's.

Everything about it was false.

Right then, in that office, with the realization that no one knew the truth about my life, my thoughts about the world were shaken.

Like driving along a bumpy road and losing control of the steering wheel, tossing you—just a tad—off the road. The wheels kick up some dirt, but you're able to pull it back. Yet no matter how tightly you grip the wheel, no matter how hard you try to drive straight, something keeps jerking you to the side. You have so little control over anything anymore. And at some point, the struggle becomes too much—too tiring—and you consider letting go. Allowing tragedy . . . or whatever . . . to happen.

Pressing my fingertips hard against my hairline, my thumbs against my temples, I squeeze.

In that picture, I'm sure Courtney was wearing a beautiful smile. Fake, but beautiful.

She wasn't. But you couldn't know that.

See, Courtney thought she could jerk me around wherever she wanted. But I didn't let that happen. I jerked myself back on the road just long enough to push her off . . . if only for a moment.

But now? The survey. For Valentine's Day. Was this just another chance to get thrown off the road? Was this survey, for the guys who found my name on their list, going to be the excuse they needed to ask me out?

And would they be extra excited about doing that because of the rumors they'd heard?

I looked at the slit in the top of the shoebox, too thin to squeeze my fingers through. But I could lift off the top and take out my survey. It'd be so easy. Ms. Benson would ask why and I could pretend I was embarrassed about filling out a love survey. She'd understand.

Or . . . I could wait and see.

If I had been smart, if I had been honest with my survey, I would have described Hannah. And maybe we would have talked. Seriously talked. Not just joking around like last summer at the movie theater.

But I didn't do that. I wasn't thinking that way.

Would most students, as I expected, get their list and just have a good laugh, thinking nothing of it? Or would they use it?

If Hannah's name and number had shown up on my list, would I have called her?

I slouch down into the cold bench, leaning my head back. Far back, like the tip of my spine might burst if I keep going.

Very little, I told myself, could go wrong. The survey was a joke. No one's going to use it. Calm down, Hannah. You are not setting yourself up.

But if I was right—if I called it correctly—if I willingly gave someone an excuse to test those rumors about me . . . well . . . I don't know. Maybe I'd shrug it off. Maybe I'd get pissed.

Or maybe I would let go and give up.

This time, for the first time, I saw the possibilities in giving up. I even found hope in it.

Ever since Kat's going-away party, I couldn't stop thinking about Hannah. How she looked. How she acted. How it never matched up with what I heard. But I was too afraid to find out for sure. Too afraid she might laugh if I asked her out.

Just too afraid.

So what were my options? I could leave the office a pessimist and take my survey with me. Or I could leave it as an optimist and hope for the best. In the end, I walked out of that office with my survey still in the box, unsure of what I was. An optimist? A pessimist?

Neither. A fool.

I close my eyes, concentrating on the cool air floating around me.

When I went into the movie theater last summer for a job application, I pretended to be surprised that Hannah worked there. But she was the whole reason I applied.

"Today's the day!" the cheerleader said . . . cheerfully, of course. "Pick up your Oh My Dollar Valentines at the student body office today."

On my first day at work, they placed me in the concession stand with Hannah. She showed me how to pump "butter" topping into the popcorn.

She said that if someone I had a crush on came in, I shouldn't put butter in the bottom half of the tub. That way, halfway through the movie, they'd come back out asking for more. And then there wouldn't be so many people around and we could talk.

But I never did that. Because it was Hannah I was interested in. And the thought that she did that for other guys made me jealous.

I hadn't decided yet if I wanted to find out who the survey matched me up with. With my luck, it'd be a fellow lumberjack. But when I walked by the office and found no one standing in line, I thought . . . what the hell.

I went up to the counter and started saying my name, but the cheerleader at the computer cut me off.

"Thanks for supporting the cheerleaders, Hannah." She tilted her head to one side and smiled. "That sounded dumb, right? But I'm supposed to say it to everyone."

It was probably the same cheerleader who gave me my survey results.

She typed my name into the computer, hit Enter, then asked how many names I wanted. One, or five? I placed a five-dollar bill on the counter. She hit the number Five key and a printer on my side of the counter spit out my list.

She told me they put the printer on our side so the cheerleaders wouldn't be tempted to peek at our names. So people wouldn't feel embarrassed by who they got.

I told her that was a good idea and started looking over my list.

"So," the cheerleader said, "who'd you get?"

Definitely the cheerleader who helped me.

She was joking, of course.

No she wasn't.

Half-joking. I placed my list on the counter for her to see.

"Not bad," she said. "Ooh, I like this one."

I agreed that it wasn't a bad list. But not wonderful, either.

She lifted her shoulders and called my list a shrugger.

Then she let me in on a little secret. It wasn't the most scientific of surveys.

Except for people seeking a depressed loner like Holden Caulfield. For that, the survey deserved a Nobel Prize.

We both agreed that two names on the list matched me fairly well. Another name, one that I was pleased with, brought an entirely different reaction out of her.

"No," she said. Her expression, her posture, lost all its cheeriness. "Trust me . . . no."

Is he on one of your tapes, Hannah? Is that who this tape is about? Because I don't think this tape is about the cheerleader.

"But he's cute," I said.

"On the outside," she told me.

She pulled out a stack of fives from the register, put mine on top, then went through the stack turning each bill the same way.

I didn't push the subject, but I should have. And in a couple more tapes you'll know why.

Which reminds me, I haven't told you who our main man on this tape is. Fortunately, this is the perfect time to introduce him because that's exactly when he showed up.

Again, not me.

Something started buzzing. A phone? I looked at the cheerleader, but she shook her head. So I swung my backpack onto the counter, fished out my phone, and answered it.

"Hannah Baker," the caller said. "Good to see you."

I looked at the cheerleader and shrugged. "Who is this?" I asked.

"Guess how I got your number," he said.

I told him that I hated guessing games, so he told me. "I paid for it."

"You paid for my phone number?"

The cheerleader scooped her hand over her mouth and pointed at the printout—the Oh My Dollar Valentines!

No way, I thought. Someone was actually calling because my name was on their list? Kind of exciting, yes. But kind of weird at the same time.

The cheerleader touched the names we both thought were good matches, but I shook my head no. I knew those voices well enough to know it wasn't either of them. It also wasn't the one she warned me about.

I read the other two names on my list out loud.

"It looks like you made my list," the caller said, "but I didn't make yours."

Actually, you did make her list. A different list. One I'm sure you don't like being on.

I asked him where on his list my name popped up.

Again, he told me to guess, then quickly added that he was joking. "Ready for this?" he asked. "You're my number one, Hannah."

I mouthed his answer—number one!—and the cheerleader hopped up and down.

"This is so cool," she whispered.

The caller then asked what I was doing for Valentine's Day.

"Depends," I told him. "Who are you?"

But he didn't answer. He didn't need to. Because at that moment, I saw him . . . standing right outside the office window. Marcus Cooley.

Hello, Marcus.

I grit my teeth. Marcus. I should've hit him with the rock when I had the chance.

Marcus, as you know, is one of the biggest goof-offs at school. Not a slacker goof-off, but a good goof-off.

Guess again.

He's actually funny. An endless number of painfully dull classes have been rescued by a perfectly timed Cooley pun. So naturally, I didn't take his words at face value.

Even though he only stood a few feet away, separated by a window, I kept talking to him through the phone. "You're lying," I said. "I am not on your list."

His normally goofy smirk, at that moment, looked kind of sexy. "What—you don't think I'm ever serious?" he asked. Then he pressed his list against the window.

Even though I stood too far away to actually read it, I assumed he'd only hold it up to prove that my name did in fact hold his top spot. Still, I thought he must've been kidding about getting together for Valentine's Day. So I thought I'd make him squirm a bit.

"Fine," I said. "When?"

The cheerleader covered her face with both hands, but through her fingers I watched her skin blush.

I don't know, without her as an audience egging me on, I doubt I would have agreed to go out with him that fast. But I was playing it up. Giving her something to brag about at cheer practice.

Now it was Marcus's turn to blush. "Oh . . . um . . . Okay . . . well . . . How about Rosie's? You know, for ice cream."

E-5. I saw that star on the map while riding the bus. I knew roughly where it was, just not which store specifically. But I should've guessed. The best ice cream and the greasiest burgers and fries around. Rosie's Diner.

My words came out sarcastic. "Ice cream?" But I didn't mean them that way. An ice cream date just sounded so . . . cute. So I agreed to meet him there after school. And with that, we hung up.

The cheerleader slapped her hands on the counter. "You have absolutely got to let me brag about this."

I made her promise not to tell anyone until the next day, just in case.

"Fine," she said. But she made me promise to spill every last detail afterward.

Some of you may know the cheerleader I've been talking about, but I'm not saying her name. She was very sweet and excited for me. She did nothing wrong.

Honestly. No sarcasm there. Don't strain yourselves reading into my words.

Before, I thought I knew who the cheerleader was. But now, remembering the day we all found out about Hannah, I'm sure of it. Jenny Kurtz. We had Biology together. By then, I'd already heard. But that's when she found out, scalpel in hand, an earthworm sliced down the middle and pinned open before her. She put down the scalpel and fell into a long, stunned silence. Then she got up and, without stopping by the teacher's desk for a pass, walked out of the room.

I kept looking for her the rest of that day, puzzled by her reaction. Like most people, I had no clue of her random connection to Hannah Baker.

Did I tell the cheerleader about what happened at Rosie's? No. Instead, I avoided her for as long as I could.

And you're about to find out why.

Of course, I couldn't avoid her forever. Which is why, in a little while, she'll make another appearance on these tapes . . . but with a name.

The cold air isn't the only reason I'm shivering anymore. With every side of every tape, an old memory gets turned upside down. A reputation twists into someone I don't recognize.

I felt like crying when I watched Jenny walk out of Biology. Every time I saw a reaction like that, with her, with Mr. Porter, it threw me back to the moment I found out about Hannah myself. When I did cry.

When instead, I should have been angry at them.

So if you want the full Hannah experience, go to Rosie's for yourself.

God. I hate not knowing what to believe anymore. I hate not knowing what's real.

E-5 on your map. Sit down on one of the stools at the counter. In a minute, I'll tell you what to do after seating yourself. But first, a little background on me and Rosie's.

I had never gone there before that day. I know, it seems crazy. Everyone's been to Rosie's. It's the cool, quirky place to hang out. But as far as I knew, no one ever went there alone. And every time someone invited me, for some reason or another, I was busy. Family visiting from out of town. Too much homework. Always something.

To me, Rosie's had an aura about it. A mystery. In the stories I heard, it seemed like things were always happening there. Alex Standall, his first week in town, had his first fight outside Rosie's front door. He told me and Jessica about it during our Monet's Garden Café period.

When I heard about that fight, it came as advice not to mess with the new kid. Alex knew how to throw, as well as take, a punch.

A girl, whose name I will not repeat, had her first under-the-bra experience at Rosie's while making out between the pinball machines.

Courtney Crimsen. Everyone knew about that. And it's not like Courtney tried to hide it.

With all the stories, it seemed that Rosie turned a blind eye to anything going on as long as cones were being filled and burgers were being flipped. So I wanted to go, but I was not about to go alone and look like a dork.

Marcus Cooley gave me the excuse I needed. And it just so happened that I was free.

Free, but not stupid.

I was a little wary of Marcus. A little suspicious. But not of him so much as the people he hung out with.

People like Alex Standall.

After peeling away from our olly-olly-oxen-free group at Monet's, Alex started hanging out with Marcus. And after the little stunt Alex pulled with the "Who's Hot / Who's Not" list, I didn't trust him.

So why would I trust someone he hangs out with?

You shouldn't.

Why? Because that's exactly what I wanted for me. I wanted people to trust me, despite anything they'd heard. And more than that, I wanted them to know me. Not the stuff they thought they knew about me. No, the real me. I wanted them to get past the rumors. To see beyond the relationships I once had, or maybe still had but that they didn't agree with. And if I wanted people to treat me that way, then I had to do the same for them, right?

So I walked into Rosie's and sat at the counter. And when you go there, if you go there, don't order right away.

The phone in my pocket starts vibrating.

Just sit and wait.

And wait a little more.

It's Mom.

II

I answer the phone, but even the simplest words catch in my throat and I say nothing.

"Honey?" Her voice is soft. "Is everything all right?"

I close my eyes to concentrate, to speak calmly. "I'm fine." But does she hear it?

"Clay, honey, it's getting late." She pauses. "Where are you?"

"I forgot to call. I'm sorry."

"It's okay." She hears it, but she won't ask. "Do you want me to pick you up?"

I can't go home. Not yet. I almost tell her I need to stay till I'm done helping Tony with his school project. But I'm almost done with this tape and I only have one more with me.

"Mom? Can you do me a favor?"

No response.

"I left some tapes on the workbench."

"For your project?"

Wait! But what if she listens to them? What if, to see

what they are, she slides a tape into the stereo? What if it's Hannah talking about me?

"It's okay. Never mind," I say. "I'll get them."

"I can bring them to you."

I don't answer. The words aren't caught in my throat, I just don't know which ones to use.

"I'm heading out anyway," she says. "We're out of bread and I'm making sandwiches for tomorrow."

I exhale a tiny laugh and I smile. Whenever I'm out late she makes a sandwich for my school lunch. I always protest and tell her not to, saying I'll make my own when I get home. But she likes it. She says it reminds her of when I was younger and needed her.

"Just tell me where you are," she says.

Leaning forward on the metal bench, I say the first thing that comes to mind. "I'm at Rosie's."

"The diner? Are you getting work done there?" She waits for an answer, but I don't have one. "Doesn't it get loud?"

The street is empty. No cars. No noise. No commotion in the background. She knows I'm not telling the truth.

"When are you going to leave?" I ask.

"As soon as I get the tapes."

"Great." I start walking. "I'll see you soon."

▶

Listen to the conversations around you. Are people wonder-

ing why you're sitting there alone? Now glance over your shoulder. Did a conversation stop? Did their eyes turn away?

I'm sorry if this sounds pathetic, but you know it's true. You've never gone there by yourself, have you?

I haven't.

It's a totally different experience. And deep down you know the reason you've never gone alone is the reason I just explained. But if you do go, and you don't order anything, everyone's going to think the same thing about you that they thought about me. That you're waiting for someone.

So sit there. And every few minutes, glance at the clock on the wall. The longer you wait—and this is true—the slower the hands will move.

Not today. When I get there, my heart will be racing as I watch the hands spin closer and closer to Mom walking through the door.

I start to run.

When fifteen minutes are up, you have my permission to order a shake. Because fifteen minutes is ten minutes longer than it should take even the slowest person to walk there from school.

Somebody . . . isn't coming.

Now, if you need a recommendation, you can't go wrong with the banana-and-peanut-butter shake.

Then keep waiting, however long it takes to finish your

shake. If thirty minutes go by, start digging in with your spoon so you can get the hell out of there. That's what I did.

You're an ass, Marcus. You stood her up when you never even had to ask her out to begin with. It was a fund-raiser for Cheer Camp. If you didn't want to take it seriously, you didn't have to.

Thirty minutes is a long time to wait for a Valentine's date. Especially inside Rosie's Diner by yourself. It also gives you plenty of time to wonder what happened. Did he forget? Because he seemed sincere. I mean, even the cheerleader thought he meant it, right?

I keep running.

Calm down, Hannah. That's what I kept telling myself. You're not setting yourself up for a fall. Calm down. Does that sound familiar to anyone else? Isn't that how I convinced myself not to pull my survey out of the box?

Okay, stop. Those were the thoughts running through my head after waiting thirty minutes for Marcus to show up. Which probably didn't put me in a good frame of mind for when he finally did show up.

My running slows. Not because I'm out of breath or my legs are ready to collapse. I'm not physically tired. But I'm exhausted.

If Marcus didn't stand her up, then what?

He sat down on the stool next to me and apologized. I told him that I'd almost given up and left. He looked at my empty milkshake glass and apologized again. But in his mind, he wasn't late. He wasn't sure I would even be there.

And I'm not going to hold that against him. Apparently, he thought we were joking about the date. Or he assumed we were joking about the date. But halfway home, he stopped, thought about it, and headed to Rosie's just in case.

And that's why you're on this tape, Marcus. You turned around just in case. Just in case I, Hannah Baker—Miss Reputation—was waiting for you.

And sadly, I was. At the time, I just thought it might be fun.

At the time, I was stupid.

There's Rosie's. Across the street. At the far end of the parking lot.

See, when Marcus came into Rosie's, he wasn't alone. No, Marcus came into Rosie's with a plan. Part of that plan was to move us away from the counter to a booth near the back. Near the pinball machines. With me on the inside.

Me, sandwiched between him . . . and a wall.

The parking lot is nearly empty. Only a few cars directly in front of Rosie's, but none of them are Mom's. So I stop.

If you want, if you're sitting at Rosie's right now, stay at the counter. It's more comfortable there. Believe me.

I stand on the curb, breathing deep, exhaling hard. A red hand flashes at the intersection across the street.

I don't know how much of his plan was thought out. Maybe he arrived with just an endgame. A goal. And like I said, Marcus is funny. So there we were, sitting in a booth with our backs to the rest of the diner, laughing. At one point Marcus had me laughing so hard that my stomach hurt. I leaned over, touching my forehead to his shoulder, begging him to stop.

The hand keeps flashing, urging me to make up my mind. Telling me to hurry. I still have time to run across the street, jump the curb, and race through the parking lot to Rosie's.

But I don't.

And that's when his hand touched my knee. That's when I knew.

The hand stops flashing. A solid, bright red hand.

And I turn around. I can't go in there. Not yet.

I stopped laughing. I nearly stopped breathing. But I kept my forehead against your shoulder, Marcus. There was your hand, on my knee. From out of nowhere. The same way I was grabbed in the liquor store.

"What are you doing?" I whispered.

"Do you want me to move it?" you asked.

I didn't answer.

I press my hand against my stomach. It's too much. Too much to handle.

I'll go to Rosie's. In a minute. And hopefully, I'll get there before Mom.

But first, the theater where Hannah and I worked for one summer. A place where she was safe: the Crestmont.

And I didn't move away from you, either.

It was like you and your shoulder weren't connected anymore. Your shoulder was just a prop to rest my head against while I figured things out. And I couldn't look away as your fingertips caressed my knee . . . and started moving up.

"Why are you doing that?" I asked.

It's only a block away, and maybe it's not a red star on her map, but it should've been.

It's a red star to me.

Your shoulder rotated and I lifted my head, but now your arm was behind my back and pulling me close. And your other hand was touching my leg. My upper thigh.

I looked over the back of the booth to the other booths, to the counter, trying to catch someone's eye. And a few people glanced over, but they all turned away.

Below the table, my fingers were fighting to pry your fingers off. To loosen your grip. To push you away. And I didn't want to yell—it wasn't to that level yet—but my eyes were begging for help.

I shove my hands in my pockets, balled into fists. I want to slam them into a wall or punch them through a store window. I've never hit anything or anyone before, and already, just tonight, I've wanted to hit Marcus with that rock.

But everyone turned away. No one asked if there was a problem.

Why? Were they being polite?

Was that it, Zach? Were you just being polite?

Zach? Again? With Justin on the first tape, falling on Hannah's lawn. Then interrupting me and Hannah at Kat's going-away party.

I hate this. I don't want to find out how everyone fits together anymore.

"Stop it," I said. And I know you heard me because, with me looking over the backrest, my mouth was just inches away from your ear. "Stop it."

The Crestmont. I round the corner and, less than half a block away, there it is. One of the few landmarks in town. The last art deco theater in the state.

"Don't worry," you said. And maybe you knew your time was short because your hand immediately slid up from my thigh. All the way up.

So I rammed both of my hands into your side, throwing you to the floor.

Now, when someone falls out of a booth, it's kind of funny. It just is. So you'd think people would've started laughing. Unless, of course, they knew it wasn't an accident. So they knew something was going on in that booth, they just didn't feel like helping.

Thanks.

The wraparound marquee stretching over the sidewalk. The ornate sign reaching to the sky like an electric peacock feather. Each letter flickers on one at a time, C-R-E-S-T-M-O-N-T, like filling in a crossword puzzle with neon letters.

Anyway, you left. You didn't storm out. Just called me a tease, loud enough for everyone to hear, and walked out.

So now, let's back up. To me, sitting at the counter, getting ready to leave. To me, thinking Marcus wasn't showing up because he simply didn't care. And I'll tell you what I was thinking then. Because now, it applies even more.

I walk toward the Crestmont. The other stores I pass are all closed for the night. A solid wall of darkened windows. But then a triangular wedge cuts away from the sidewalk, its walls and marble floor the same colors as the neon sign, pointing in to the lobby. And in the middle of the wedge, the box office. Like a tollbooth, with windows on three sides and a door in the rear.

That's where I worked on most nights.

For the longest time, from almost day one at this school, it seemed that I was the only one who cared about me.

Put all of your heart into getting that first kiss . . . only to have it thrown back in your face.

Have the only two people you truly trust turn against you.

Have one of them use you to get back at the other, and then be accused of betrayal.

Are you getting it now? Am I going too fast?

Well, keep up!

Let someone take away any sense of privacy or security you might still possess. Then have someone use that insecurity to satisfy their own twisted curiosity.

She pauses. Slows down a bit.

Then come to realize that you're making mountains out of molehills. Realize how petty you've become. Sure, it may feel like you can't get a grip in this town. It may seem that every time someone offers you a hand up, they just let go and you slip further down. But you must stop being so pessimistic, Hannah, and learn to trust those around you.

So I do. One more time.

The last movie of the night is playing, so the box office is empty. I stand on the swirling marbled floor, surrounded by posters of coming attractions.

This was my chance, at this theater, to reach Hannah.

It was my chance and I let it slip away.

And then . . . well . . . certain thoughts begin creeping around. Will I ever get control of my life? Will I always be shoved back and pushed around by those I trust?

I hate what you did, Hannah.

Will my life ever go where I want it to?

You didn't have to do it and I hate the fact that you did.

The next day, Marcus, I decided something. I decided to find out how people at school might react if one of the students never came back.

As the song goes, "You are lost and gone forever, oh my darling, Valentine."

I lean back against a poster locked behind a plastic frame and I close my eyes.

I'm listening to someone give up. Someone I knew. Someone I liked.

I'm listening. But still, I'm too late.

■

My heart is pounding and I can't stand still. I walk across the marble floor to the box office. A small sign hangs by a chain and a tiny suction cup. CLOSED—SEE YOU TOMORROW! From out here, it doesn't look so cramped. But in there, it felt like a fishbowl.

My only interaction came when people slid money over to my side of the glass and I slid back their tickets. Or when a coworker let themselves in through the rear door.

Other than that, if I wasn't selling tickets, I was reading. Or staring out of the fishbowl, into the lobby, watching Hannah. And some nights were worse than others. Some nights I watched to make sure she buttered the popcorn all the way through. Which seems silly now, and obsessive, but that's what I did.

Like the night Bryce Walker came. He arrived with his girlfriend-of-the-moment and wanted me to charge her the under-twelve rate.

"She won't be watching the movie anyway," he said. "You know what I mean, Clay?" Then he laughed.

I didn't know her. She might've been a student from another school. One thing was clear, she didn't seem to think it was funny. She placed her purse on the counter. "I'll pay for my own ticket, then."

Bryce moved her purse aside and paid the full amount. "Just relax," he told her. "It was a joke."

About halfway through the movie, while I sold tickets for the next show, that girl came tearing out of the theater holding her wrist. Maybe crying. And Bryce was nowhere to be seen.

I kept watching the lobby, waiting for him to show. But he never did. He stayed behind to finish watching the movie he had paid for.

But when the movie was over, he leaned against the concession counter, talking Hannah's ear off as everyone else left. And he stayed there while the new people came in. Hannah filled drink orders, handed out candy, gave back change, and laughed at Bryce. Laughed at whatever he said.

The entire time, I wanted to flip the Closed sign over. I wanted to march into the lobby and ask him to leave. The movie was over and he didn't need to be here anymore.

But that was Hannah's job. She should have asked him to leave. No, she should have wanted him to leave.

After selling my last ticket and turning over the sign, I

exited through the box office door, locked it behind me, and went into the lobby. To help Hannah clean up. To ask about Bryce.

"Why do you think that girl ran out of here like that?" I asked.

Hannah stopped wiping the counter and looked me straight in the eye. "I know who he is, Clay. I know what he's like. Believe me."

"I know," I said. I looked down and touched a carpet stain with the toe of my shoe. "I was just wondering, then, why'd you keep talking to him?"

She didn't answer. Not right away.

But I couldn't raise my eyes to face her. I didn't want to see a look of disappointment or frustration in her eyes. I didn't want to see those kinds of emotions directed at me.

Eventually, she said the words that ran through my mind the rest of that night: "You don't need to watch out for me, Clay."

But I did, Hannah. And I wanted to. I could have helped you. But when I tried, you pushed me away.

I can almost hear Hannah's voice speaking my next thought for me. "Then why didn't you try harder?"

CASSETTE 4: SIDE A

On my way back, the red hand flashes, but I run through the crosswalk anyway. The parking lot holds even fewer cars than before. But still, no Mom's.

A few doors down from Rosie's Diner, I stop running. I lean my back against a pet store window, trying to catch my breath. Then I lean forward, hands on my knees, hoping to slow everything down before she arrives.

Impossible. Because even though my legs stopped running, my mind keeps going. I let myself slide down against the cold glass, knees bent, trying so hard to hold back tears.

But time's running out. She'll be here soon.

Drawing in a full breath, I push myself up, walk over to Rosie's, and pull open the door.

Warm air rushes out, smelling like a mixture of hamburger grease and sugar. Inside, three of the five booths along the wall are taken. One with a boy and a girl drinking milkshakes and munching popcorn from the Crestmont. The other two are filled with students studying. Textbooks cover the tabletops, leaving just enough room for drinks and a couple of baskets of fries. Thankfully, the booth farthest back is occupied. It's not a question I need to consider, whether to sit there or not.

Taped to one of the pinball machines is a hand-scribbled Out of Order sign. A senior I sort of recognize stands in front of the other machine, banging away.

As Hannah suggested, I sit at the empty counter.

Behind the counter, a man in a white apron sorts silverware into two plastic tubs. He gives me a nod. "Whenever you're ready."

I slide a menu out from between two silver napkin holders. The front of the menu tells a lengthy story about Rosie's, with black-and-white photos spanning the last four decades. I flip it over, but nothing on the menu looks good to me. Not now.

Fifteen minutes. That's how long Hannah said to wait. Fifteen minutes and then I should order.

Something was wrong when Mom called. Something was wrong with me, and I know she heard it in my voice. But on her way over, will she listen to the tapes to find out why?

I am such an idiot. I should have told her I would go get them. But I didn't do that, so now I have to wait and find out.

The boy who was eating popcorn asks for a key to the bathroom. The man behind the counter points to the wall. Two keys hang from brass hooks. One key has a blue plastic dog attached to it. The other, a pink elephant. He grabs the blue dog and heads down the hall.

After storing the plastic tubs beneath the counter, the man unscrews the tops to a dozen salt and pepper shakers, paying no attention to me. And that's fine.

"Did you order yet?"

I swivel around. Mom sits on the stool next to me and pulls out a menu. Beside her, on the counter, is Hannah's shoebox.

"Are you staying?" I ask.

If she stays, we can talk. I don't mind. It would be nice to free my thoughts for a while. To take a break.

She looks me in the eyes and smiles. Then she places a hand over her stomach and forces her smile into a frown. "That's a bad idea, I think."

"You're not fat, Mom."

She slides the box of tapes over to me. "Where's your friend? Weren't you working with someone?"

Right. A school project. "He had to, you know, he's in the bathroom."

Her eyes look past me, over my shoulder, for just a second.

And I might be wrong, but I think she checked to see if both keys were hanging on the wall.

Thank God they weren't.

"Did you bring enough money?" she asks.

"For?"

"For something to eat." She replaces her menu then taps a fingernail against my menu. "The chocolate malteds are to die for."

"You've eaten here?" I'm a little surprised. I've never seen adults in Rosie's before.

Mom laughs. She places a hand on top of my head and uses her thumb to smooth out the wrinkles on my forehead. "Don't look so amazed, Clay. This place has been around forever." She pulls out a ten-dollar bill and lays it on top of the shoebox. "Have what you want, but have a malted shake for me."

When she stands, the bathroom door squeaks open. I turn my head and watch the guy rehang the blue dog key. He apologizes to his girlfriend for taking so long and kisses her on the forehead before sitting down.

"Clay?" Mom says.

Before turning back around, I shut my eyes for just a moment, and breathe. "Yes?"

She forces a smile. "Don't be out long." But it's a hurt smile.

Four tapes remain. Seven stories. And still, where is my name?

I look into her eyes. "It might be a while." Then I look down. At the menu. "It's a school project."

She says nothing, but from the corner of my eye I can see her standing there. She lifts a hand. I close my eyes and feel her fingers touch the top of my head then slide down to the back of my neck.

"Be careful," she says.

I nod.

And she leaves.

I take the top off the shoebox and unroll the bubble-wrap. The tapes haven't been touched.

▶

Everyone's favorite class . . . okay, everyone's favorite required *class . . . is Peer Communications. It's kind of the nonelective elective. Everyone would take it even if it wasn't required because it's such an easy A.*

And most of the time, it's fun. I'd take it just for that.

There's very little homework, and don't forget the bonus points for class participation. I mean, they encourage you to yell out in class. What's not to like?

Reaching down, I grab my backpack and lift it onto the stool where Mom sat only moments ago.

After feeling more and more like an outcast, Peer Communications was my safe haven at school. Whenever I walked into that room, I felt like throwing open my arms and shouting, "Olly-olly-oxen-free!"

I roll the three tapes I've already heard into the bubble-wrap and place them back in the shoebox. Finished. Done.

For one period each day, you were not allowed to touch me or snicker behind my back no matter what the latest rumor. Mrs. Bradley did not appreciate people who snickered.

I unzip the largest pocket of my backpack and stow Hannah's shoebox inside it.

That was rule number one, day number one. If anyone snickered at what anyone else said, they owed Mrs. Bradley a Snickers bar. And if it was an extremely rude snicker, you owed her a King Size.

On the counter, sitting beside the Walkman and a chocolate malted shake in honor of Mom, are the next three tapes.

And everyone paid up without argument. That's the kind of respect people had for Mrs. Bradley. No one accused her of picking on them, because she never did. If she said you snickered, you did. And you knew it. The next day, there would be a Snickers bar waiting on her desk.

And if there wasn't? I don't know.

There always was.

I gather the next two tapes, blue nail polish labeling them nine and ten, eleven and twelve, and hide them in my inside jacket pocket.

Mrs. Bradley said Peer Communications was her favorite class to teach—or moderate, as she called it. Each day, we had a brief reading assignment full of statistics and real-world examples. Then, we discussed.

The last tape, the seventh tape, has a thirteen on one side but nothing on the reverse. I slip this tape into the back pocket of my jeans.

Bullies. Drugs. Self-image. Relationships. Everything was fair game in Peer Communications. Which, of course, made a lot of other teachers upset. It was a waste of time, they said. They wanted to teach us cold hard facts. They understood cold hard facts.

Headlights flash across Rosie's front window and I squint while they pass.

They wanted to teach us the meaning of x *in relation to pi, as opposed to helping us better understand ourselves and each other. They wanted us to know when the Magna Carta was signed—never mind what it was—as opposed to discussing birth control.*

We have Sex Ed., but that's a joke.

Which meant that each year, during budget meetings, Peer Communications was on the chopping block. And each year, Mrs. Bradley and the other teachers brought a bunch of students to the school board with examples of how we benefited from the class.

Okay, I could go on like this forever, defending Mrs. Bradley. But something happened in that class, didn't it? Otherwise, why would you be listening to me talk about it?

Next year, after my little incident, I hope Peer Communications continues.

I know, I know. You thought I was going to say something else, didn't you? You thought I was going to say that if the class played a part in my decision, it should be cut. But it shouldn't.

No one at school knows what I'm about to tell you. And it wasn't really the class itself that played a part. Even if I never took Peer Communications, the outcome may very well have been the same.

Or not.

I guess that's the point of it all. No one knows for certain how much impact they have on the lives of other people. Oftentimes, we have no clue. Yet we push it just the same.

Mom was right. The shake is amazing. A perfect blend of ice cream and chocolate malt.

And I'm a jerk for sitting here, enjoying it.

At the back of Mrs. Bradley's room stood a wire bookrack. The kind you spin. The kind that holds paperback novels in the supermarket. But this rack never held any books. Instead, at the beginning of the year, each student received a paper lunch bag to decorate with crayons and stickers and stamps. Then we opened our bags and hung them to the rack with a couple of pieces of tape.

Mrs. Bradley knew people had a difficult time saying nice things to each other, so she devised a way for us to anonymously say what we felt.

Did you admire the way so-and-so talked openly about his family? Drop a note in his bag and tell him.

Do you understand so-and-so's concern about not passing history? Drop her a note. Tell her you'll think about her as you study for the upcoming test.

Did you like his performance in the school play?

Do you like her new haircut?

She got a haircut. In the photo at Monet's, Hannah's hair was long. That's how I always picture it. Even now. But that's not how it was at the end.

If you can, tell them to their face. But if you can't, drop them a note and they'll feel it just the same. And as far as I know, no one ever left a mean or sarcastic note in anyone's bag. We had too much respect for Mrs. Bradley to do that.

So, Zach Dempsey, what's your excuse?

II

What? What happened?

Oh God. I look up to find Tony standing beside me, his finger on the Pause button.

"Is this my Walkman?"

I don't say anything, because I can't read his expression. It's not anger, even though I did steal his Walkman.

Confusion? Maybe. But if it is, it's more than that. It's the same look he gave when I helped him with his car. When he was watching me instead of shining the flashlight for his dad.

Worry. Concern.

"Tony, hey."

I pull the headphones from my ears and slip them around my neck. The Walkman. Right, he asked about the Walkman. "It is. It was in your car. I saw it when I was helping you. Earlier today. I think I asked if I could borrow it."

I'm such an idiot.

He rests a hand on top of the counter and sits on the stool next to me. "I'm sorry, Clay," he says. He looks into my eyes. Can he tell I'm a horrible liar? "I get so frustrated around my dad sometimes. I'm sure you asked and I just forgot."

His gaze falls to the yellow headphones around my neck, then follows the long cord to the tape deck on the counter. I pray that he doesn't ask what I'm listening to.

Between Tony and my mom, I'm doing a lot of lying today. And if he does ask, I'll need to do it again.

"Just return it when you're done," he says. He stands and places a hand on my shoulder. "Keep it as long as you need."

"Thanks."

"No need to rush," he says. He grabs a menu from between the napkin holders, walks to an empty booth behind me, and sits down.

▶

Don't worry, Zach. You never left anything mean in my

bag. I know that. But what you did do, was worse.

From what I know, Zach's a good guy. Too shy for people to even want to gossip about.

And like me, he's always had a thing for Hannah Baker.

But first, let's go back a few weeks. Let's go back . . . to Rosie's.

My stomach pulls in tight, like working through a final sit-up. I close my eyes and concentrate on bringing myself back to normal. But I haven't felt normal in hours. Even the lids of my eyes feel warm. Like my whole body is fighting a sickness.

I just sat there, in the booth where Marcus left me, staring into an empty milkshake glass. His side of the bench was probably still warm because he'd left only a minute ago. When up walked Zach.

And down he sat.

I open my eyes to the row of empty stools on this side of the counter. On one of these stools, maybe this one, Hannah sat when she first arrived. By herself. But then Marcus arrived and took her to a booth.

My gaze follows the counter down to the pinball machines at the far end of the diner, then over to their booth. Empty.

I pretended not to notice him. Not because I had anything against him, but because my heart and my trust were in the process of collapsing. And that collapse created a vacuum in my chest. Like every nerve in my body was withering in, pulling away from my fingers and toes. Pulling back and disappearing.

My eyes burn. I reach forward and slide a hand down the frosted milkshake glass. Ice-cold droplets cling to my skin and I run my wet fingers across my eyelids.

I sat. And I thought. And the more I thought, connecting the events in my life, the more my heart collapsed.

Zach was sweet. He went on letting me ignore him until it became almost comical. I knew he was there, of course. He was practically staring at me. And eventually, melodramatically, he cleared his throat.

I lifted my hand onto the table and touched the base of my glass. That was the only sign he was going to get that I was listening.

I pull my glass closer and turn the spoon inside it in slow circles, softening whatever remains at the bottom.

He asked if I was all right, and I forced myself to nod. But my eyes kept staring at the glass—through the glass—at the spoon. And I kept thinking, over and over, Is this what it feels like to go insane?

"I'm sorry," he said. "For whatever happened just now."

I felt my head continue to nod as if it was attached to heavy springs, but I couldn't bring myself to tell him that I appreciated his words.

He offered to buy me another milkshake, but I gave no response. Was I unable to talk? Or did I just not want to talk? I don't know. Part of me thought he was hitting on me—ready to use the fact that I was now alone to ask me out. And it's not that I completely believed that, but why should I trust him?

The waitress dropped off my bill and took the empty glass away. Soon, getting nothing out of me, Zach left a few bucks on the table and returned to his friends.

I keep stirring my malted. There's hardly any left, but I don't want the glass taken away. It gives me a reason to sit here. To stay here.

My eyes began tearing up, but I could not break my stare from the small wet circle where the glass had been. If I even tried to utter a single word, I would have lost it.

Or had I already lost it?

I keep stirring.

I can tell you this, at that table, the worst thoughts in the world first came into my head. It's there that I first started to consider . . . to consider . . . a word that I still cannot say.

I know you tried coming to my rescue, Zach. But we all know that's not why you're on this tape. So I've got one question before we continue. When you try rescuing someone and discover they can't be reached, why would you ever throw that back in their face?

For the past several days or weeks or however long it took you to get these tapes, Zach, you probably thought no one would find out.

I lower my face into my hands. How many secrets can there be at one school?

You probably got sick to your stomach when you heard what I did. But the more time that went by, the better you felt. Because the more time that went by, the more likely your secret died with me. No one knew. No one would ever find out.

But now we will. And my stomach gets a little sicker.

Let me ask you, Zach, did you think I turned you down at Rosie's? I mean, you never got around to asking me out, so I couldn't officially turn you down, right? So what was it? Embarrassment?

Let me guess. You told your friends to watch while you put the moves on me . . . and then I hardly responded.

Or was it a dare? Did they dare you to ask me out?

People did that. Recently someone dared me to ask Hannah out. He worked with both of us at the Crestmont. He knew I liked her and that I never found the nerve to ask her out. He also knew that for the past few months, Hannah hardly spoke to anyone, making it a double challenge.

When I broke out of my daze, and before I left, I listened in on you and your friends. They were teasing you for not getting that date you assured them was in the bag.

I will give you credit where it's due, Zach. You could have gone back to your friends and said, "Hannah's a freak. Look at her. She's staring into Neverland."

Instead, you took the teasing.

But you must have a slow boil, getting more and more angry—taking it more and more personally—the longer you thought about my nonresponsiveness. And you chose to get back at me in the most childish of ways.

You stole my paper bag notes of encouragement.

How pathetic.

So what tipped me off? It's simple, really. Everyone else was getting notes. Everyone! And for the most insignificant of things. Anytime someone even got a haircut they got a bunch of notes. And there were people in that class I considered friends who would have put something in my bag after I chopped off most of my hair.

When she first walked by me in the halls, with her hair cut so much shorter, I couldn't keep my mouth from falling open. And she looked away. Out of habit, she tried brushing the hair out of her face and behind her ears. But it was too short and kept falling forward.

Come to think of it, I cut my hair the very day Marcus Cooley and I met at Rosie's.

Wow! That's weird. All those warning signs they tell us to watch out for, they're true. I went straight from Rosie's to get my hair cut. I needed a change, just like they said, so I changed my appearance. The only thing I still had control over.

Amazing.

She pauses. Silence. Just static, barely audible, in the headphones.

I'm sure the school had psychologists come in loaded with handouts, telling you what to look for in students who might be considering . . .

Another pause.

No. Like I said before, I can't say it.

Suicide. Such a disgusting word.

The next day, when I found my bag empty, I knew something was up. At least, I thought something was up. The first few months of class I received maybe four or five notes. But suddenly, after the telltale haircut . . . nothing.

So after my haircut, I waited a week.

Then two weeks.

Then three weeks.

Nothing.

I push my glass across the counter and look at the man down by the register. "Can you take this?"

It was time to find out what was going on. So I wrote myself a note.

He shoots me a hard look while counting back change. The girl on this side of the register also looks at me. She touches her ears. The headphones. I'm speaking too loud.

"Sorry," I whisper. Or maybe it doesn't come out at all.

"Hannah," the note said. "Like the new haircut. Sorry I didn't tell you sooner." And for good measure, I added a purple smiley face.

To avoid the major embarrassment of getting caught leaving myself a note, I also wrote a note for the bag next to mine. And after class, I walked to the bookrack and made a show of dropping a note in that other bag. Then I casually ran my hand around the inside of my bag, pretending to check for notes. And I say "pretending" because I knew it would be empty.

And the next day? Nothing in my bag. The note was gone.

Maybe it didn't seem like a big deal to you, Zach. But now, I hope you understand. My world was collapsing. I needed those notes. I needed any hope those notes might have offered.

And you? You took that hope away. You decided I didn't deserve to have it.

The longer I listen to these tapes, the more I feel I know her. Not the Hannah from the past few years, but the one from the past few months. That's the Hannah I'm beginning to understand.

Hannah at the end.

The last time I found myself this close to a person, a person slowly dying, was the night of the party. The night I watched two cars collide in a dark intersection.

Then, like now, I didn't know they were dying.

Then, like now, there were a lot of people around. But what could they have done? Those people standing around the car, trying to calm the driver, waiting for an ambulance to arrive, could they have done anything at all?

Or the people who passed Hannah in the halls, or sat beside her in class, what could they have done?

Maybe then, like now, it was already too late.

So Zach, how many notes did you take? How many notes were there that I never got to read? And did you read them? I hope so. At least someone should know what people really think of me.

I glance over my shoulder. Tony's still there, chewing a french fry and pumping ketchup on a hamburger.

I admit, during class discussions I didn't open up much. But when I did, did anyone thank me by dropping a note in my bag? That would have been nice to know. In fact, it might have encouraged me to open up even more.

This isn't fair. If Zach had any idea what Hannah was going through, I'm sure he wouldn't have stolen her notes.

The day my self-written note went missing, I stood outside the classroom door and started talking to someone I'd never spoken with before. I looked over her shoulder every few seconds, watching the other students check their bags for notes.

That sure looked like a lot of fun, Zach.

And that's when I caught you. With a single finger, you touched the lip of my bag and tilted it down just enough to peek inside.

Nothing.

So you headed toward the door without checking your own bag, which I found very interesting.

The man behind the counter picks up my glass and, with a chocolate-stained rag, wipes the counter.

Of course, that didn't prove anything. Maybe you just liked seeing who was getting notes and who wasn't . . . with a particular interest in me.

So the next day, I came into Mrs. Bradley's room during lunch. I took my paper bag off the rack and reattached it with the tiniest sliver of tape. Inside, I placed a little note folded in half.

Again, when class was over, I waited outside and watched. But I didn't talk to anyone this time. I just watched.

The perfect setup.

You touched the lip of my bag, saw the note, and reached in. The bag fell to the floor and your face turned bright red. But you bent down and scooped it up anyway. And my reaction? Disbelief. I mean, I saw it. I expected it, even. But I still couldn't believe it.

While my original plan called for me to confront you right then and there, I jumped to the side—out of the doorway.

In a hurry, you rounded the corner . . . and there we were. Face-to-face. My eyes stung as I stared at you. Then I broke that stare and lowered my head. And you took off down the hall.

She didn't want him to explain. There was no explanation. She saw it with her own eyes.

When you were halfway down the hall, still walking fast, I saw you look down as if reading something. My note? Yes.

You turned for just a moment to see if I was watching. And for that moment, I was scared. Would you confront me and tell me you were sorry? Yell at me?

The answer? None of the above. You just turned and kept walking, getting closer and closer to the doors leading outside, closer to your escape.

And as I stood there in the hallway—alone—trying to understand what had just happened and why, I realized the truth: I wasn't worth an explanation—not even a reaction. Not in your eyes, Zach.

She pauses.

For the rest of you listening, the note was addressed to Zach by name. Maybe he sees it now as a prologue to these tapes. Because in there, I admitted that I was at a point in my life where I really could have used any encouragement anyone might have left me. Encouragement . . . that he stole.

I bite on my thumb, calming the urge to look over my shoulder at Tony. Does he wonder what I'm listening to? Does he care?

But I couldn't take it anymore. You see, Zach's not the only one with a slow boil.

I shouted after him, "Why?"

In the hallway, there were still a few people changing classes. All of them jumped. But only one of them stopped.

And he stood there, facing me, cramming my note in his back pocket.

I screamed that word over and over again. Tears, finally spilling over, ran down my face. "Why? Why, Zach?"

I heard about that. Hannah flipping out for no apparent reason, embarrassing herself in front of so many people.

But they were wrong. There was a reason.

So now, let's get personal. In the spirit of opening up—of full disclosure—let me offer you this: My parents love me. I know they do. But things have not been easy recently. Not for about a year. Not since you-know-what opened outside of town.

I remember that. Hannah's parents were on the news every night, warning that if the huge shopping center went up, it would put the downtown stores out of business. They said no one would shop there anymore.

When that happened, my parents became distant. There was suddenly a lot for them to think about. A lot of pressure to make ends meet. I mean, they talked to me, but not like before.

When I cut my hair, my mom didn't even notice.

And as far as I knew—thank you, Zach—no one at school noticed, either.

I noticed.

In the back of our class, Mrs. Bradley also had a paper bag. It hung with the rest of ours on the spinning bookrack.

We could use it—and she encouraged it—for notes about her teaching. Critical or otherwise. She also wanted us to recommend topics for future discussions.

So I did just that. I wrote a note to Mrs. Bradley that read: "Suicide. It's something I've been thinking about. Not too seriously, but I have been thinking about it."

That's the note. Word for word. And I know it's word for word because I wrote it dozens of times before delivering it. I'd write it, throw it away, write it, crumple it up, throw it away.

But why was I writing it to begin with? I asked myself that question every time I printed the words onto a new sheet of paper. Why was I writing this note? It was a lie. I hadn't been thinking about it. Not really. Not in detail. The thought would come into my head and I'd push it away.

But I pushed it away a lot.

And it was a subject we never discussed in class. But I was sure more people than just me had thought about it, right? So why not discuss it as a group?

Or deep down, maybe there was more. Maybe I wanted someone to figure out who wrote the note and secretly come to my rescue.

Maybe. I don't know. But I was careful never to give myself away.

The haircut. Averting your eyes in the halls. You were careful, but still, there were signs. Little signs. But they were there.

And then, just like that, you snapped back.

Except I did give myself away to you, Zach. You knew I wrote that note in Mrs. Bradley's bag. You had to. She took it out of her bag and read it the day after I caught you. The day after I had that meltdown in the hall.

A few days before she took the pills, Hannah was herself again. She said hello to everyone in the halls. She looked us in the eyes. It seemed so drastic because it had been months since she had acted like that. Like the real Hannah.

But you did nothing, Zach. Even after Mrs. Bradley brought it up, you did nothing to reach out.

It seemed so drastic, because it was.

So what did I want from the class? Mainly, I wanted to hear what everyone had to say. Their thoughts. Their feelings.

And boy, did they tell me.

One person said it was going to be hard to help without knowing why the person wanted to kill himself.

And yes, I refrained from saying, "Or herself. It could be a girl."

Then others started chiming in.

"If they're lonely, we could invite them to sit with us at lunch."

"If it's grades, we can tutor them."

"If it's their home life, maybe we can . . . I don't know . . . get them counseling or something."

But everything they said—everything!—came tinged with annoyance.

Then one of the girls, her name doesn't matter here, said

what everyone else was thinking. "It's like whoever wrote this note just wants attention. If they were serious, they would have told us who they were."

God. There was no way for Hannah to open up in that class.

I couldn't believe it.

In the past, Mrs. Bradley had notes dropped in her bag suggesting group discussions on abortion, family violence, cheating—on boyfriends, girlfriends, on tests. No one insisted on knowing who wrote those topics. But for some reason, they refused to have a discussion on suicide without specifics.

For ten minutes or so, Mrs. Bradley rattled off statistics—local statistics—that surprised us all. Because we're juveniles, she said, as long as the suicide didn't occur in a public place with witnesses, they probably wouldn't report it in the news. And no parent wants people to know that their child, the child they raised, took his, or her, own life. So people are oftentimes led to believe it was an accident. The downside being that no one knows what's really going on with the people in their community.

That said, a thorough discussion did not begin in our class.

Were they just being nosy, or did they really think that knowing specifics was the best way to help? I'm not sure. A little of both, maybe.

In first period, Mr. Porter's class, I watched her a lot. If the topic of suicide came up, maybe our eyes would have met and I would have seen it.

And truthfully, I don't know what they could have said to sway me either way. Because maybe I was being selfish. Maybe I was just looking for attention. Maybe I just wanted to hear people discuss me and my problems.

Based on what she told me at the party, she would have wanted me to see it. She would have looked directly at me, praying for me to see it.

Or maybe I wanted someone to point a finger at me and say, "Hannah. Are you thinking about killing yourself? Please don't do that, Hannah. Please?"

But deep down, the truth was that the only person saying that was me. Deep down, those were my words.

At the end of class, Mrs. Bradley passed out a flyer called The Warning Signs of a Suicidal Individual. *Guess what was right up there in the top five?*

"A sudden change in appearance."

I tugged on the ends of my newly cropped hair.

Huh. Who knew I was so predictable?

■

Rubbing my chin against my shoulder, I see Tony out of the corner of my eye, still sitting in his booth. His hamburger's all gone, as are most of his fries. He sits there completely unaware of what I'm going through.

I open the Walkman, pop out tape number four, and flip it over.

CASSETTE 4: SIDE B

▶

Would you want the ability to hear other people's thoughts?

Of course you would. Everyone answers yes to that question, until they think it all the way through.

For example, what if other people could hear your thoughts? What if they could hear your thoughts . . . right now?

They'd hear confusion. Frustration. Even some anger. They'd hear the words of a dead girl running through my head. A girl who, for some reason, blames me for her suicide.

Sometimes we have thoughts that even we don't understand. Thoughts that aren't even true—that aren't really how we feel—but they're running through our heads anyway because they're interesting to think about.

I adjust the napkin holder in front of me till Tony's booth

is reflected in the polished silver. He leans back and wipes his hands on a napkin.

If you could hear other people's thoughts, you'd overhear things that are true as well as things that are completely random. And you wouldn't know one from the other. It'd drive you insane. What's true? What's not? A million ideas, but what do they mean?

I have no idea what Tony's thinking. And he has no idea about me. He has no idea that the voice in my head, the voice coming through his Walkman, belongs to Hannah Baker.

That's what I love about poetry. The more abstract, the better. The stuff where you're not sure what the poet's talking about. You may have an idea, but you can't be sure. Not a hundred percent. Each word, specifically chosen, could have a million different meanings. Is it a stand-in—a symbol—for another idea? Does it fit into a larger, more hidden, metaphor?

This is the eighth person, Hannah. If it's about poetry, then it's not about me. And there are only five names to go.

I hated poetry until someone showed me how to appreciate it. He told me to see poetry as a puzzle. It's up to the reader to decipher the code, or the words, based on everything they know about life and emotions.

Did the poet use red to symbolize blood? Anger? Lust? Or is the wheelbarrow simply red because red sounded better than black?

I remember that one. From English. There was a big discussion on the meaning of red. I have no idea what we decided in the end.

The same person who taught me to appreciate poetry also taught me the value in writing it. And honestly, there is no better way to explore your emotions than with poetry.

Or audiotapes.

If you're angry, you don't have to write a poem dealing with the cause of your anger. But it needs to be an angry poem. So go ahead . . . write one. I know you're at least a little bit angry with me.

And when you're done with your poem, decipher it as if you'd just found it printed in a textbook and knew absolutely nothing about its author. The results can be amazing . . . and scary. But it's always cheaper than a therapist.

I did that for a while. Poetry, not a therapist.

Maybe a therapist would have helped, Hannah.

I bought a spiral notebook to keep all of my poems in one place. A couple days a week, after school, I'd go to Monet's and write a poem or two.

My first few attempts were a bit sad. Not much depth or subtlety. Pretty straightforward. But still, some came out fairly well. At least, I think they did.

Then, without even trying, I memorized the very first poem in that notebook. And no matter how hard I try, I can't seem to shake it from my head even today. So here it is, for your appreciation . . . or amusement.

If my love were an ocean,
there would be no more land.
If my love were a desert,
you would see only sand.
If my love were a star—
late at night, only light.
And if my love could grow wings,
I'd be soaring in flight.

Go ahead. Laugh. But you know you'd buy it if you saw it on a greeting card.

There's a sudden ache deep inside my chest.

Just knowing I'd be going to Monet's to write poetry made the days more bearable. Something funny, shocking, or hurtful might happen and I'd think, This is going to make for one fascinating poem.

Over my shoulder, I see Tony walking out the front door. Which seems weird.

Why didn't he stop to say good-bye?

To me, I suppose, these tapes are a form of poetic therapy.

Through the front window, I watch Tony get in his car.

As I tell you these stories, I'm discovering certain things. Things about myself, yes, but also about you. All of you.

He flips on the headlights.

And the closer we get to the end, the more connections I'm discovering. Deep connections. Some that I've told you about, linking one story to the next. While others, I haven't told you about at all.

The Mustang shudders as Tony revs the engine. Then slowly, his car backs up.

Maybe you've even discovered some connections that I haven't. Maybe you're one step ahead of the poet.

No, Hannah. I'm barely keeping up.

And when I say my final words . . . well, probably not my final words, but the last words on these tapes . . . it's going to be one tight, well-connected, emotional ball of words.

In other words, a poem.

Watching Tony's car through the window is like watching a movie, the Mustang backing slowly offscreen. But the headlights don't gradually fade away, which they should if he kept backing up or turned away. Instead, they just stop.

As if turned off.

Looking back, I stopped writing in my notebook when I stopped wanting to know myself anymore.

Is he out there, sitting in his car, waiting? Why?

If you hear a song that makes you cry and you don't want to cry anymore, you don't listen to that song anymore.

But you can't get away from yourself. You can't decide not to see yourself anymore. You can't decide to turn off the noise in your head.

II

With Tony's headlights turned off, the windows of the diner

are just a stretch of black glass. Every so often, at the far end of the parking lot, a car drives down the road and a sliver of light glides from one end of the glass to the other.

But the only steady source of illumination, though distant, appears in the upper right-hand corner. A blurry pink-and-blue light. The tip of the Crestmont's neon sign peeking over the rooftops of every business around it.

God. What I wouldn't give to relive that summer.

When we were alone, it was so easy to talk to Hannah. It was so easy to laugh with her. But whenever people came around, I got shy. I backed off. I didn't know how to act anymore.

In that tiny fishbowl box office, my only connection to my coworkers in the lobby was a red phone. No buttons to punch, just a receiver. But whenever I picked it up and Hannah answered on the other end, I got nervous. As if I wasn't calling from thirty feet away, but calling her at home.

"I need change," I would say.

"Again?" she'd respond. But always with a smile in her voice. And every time, I felt my face grow warm with embarrassment. Because the truth was, I asked for change a lot more when she was working than when she wasn't.

A couple of minutes later, there'd be a knock on the door and I'd straighten my shirt and let her in. With a tiny cash box in hand, she'd squeeze by me, agonizingly close, to change some of my bills. And sometimes, on slow nights, she would sit in my chair and tell me to close the door.

Whenever she said that, I struggled to keep my imagination in check. Because even though windows kept us exposed on three sides, like attractions in a carnival show, and even though she only said it because we weren't supposed to leave the door open, anything could happen within that cramped space.

Or so I wished.

Those moments, however brief and rare, made me feel so special. Hannah Baker chose to spend her free moments with me. And because we were at work, no one would think anything of it. No one could read into it.

But why? Why, whenever anyone saw us, did I pretend it meant nothing? We were working, that's what I wanted them to believe. Not hanging out. Just working.

Why?

Because Hannah had a reputation. A reputation that scared me.

That truth first came to light a few weeks ago, at a party, with Hannah directly in front of me. An amazing moment when everything seemed to be falling in place.

Looking down into her eyes, I couldn't help telling her I was sorry. Sorry for waiting so long to let her know how I felt.

For a brief moment, I was able to admit it. To her. To myself. But I could never admit it again. Till now.

But now, it's too late.

And that's why, right at this moment, I feel so much hate. Toward myself. I deserve to be on this list. Because if I hadn't been so afraid of everyone else, I might have told Hannah that someone cared. And Hannah might still be alive.

I pull my gaze back from the neon sign.

▶

Sometimes I would stop by Monet's for a hot chocolate on my way home. I'd start my homework. Or sometimes I'd read. But I wasn't writing poetry anymore.

I needed a break . . . from myself.

I slide my hand from under my chin to the back of my neck. The bottom strands of my hair are drenched in sweat.

But I loved poetry. I missed it. And one day, after several weeks, I decided to go back to it. I decided to use poetry to make myself happy.

Happy poems. Bright and happy sunshiny poems. Happy, happy, happy. Like the two women pictured on the flyer at Monet's.

They taught a free course called Poetry: To Love Life. They promised to teach not only how to love poetry, but through poetry, how to better love ourselves.

Sign me up!

D-7 on your map. The community room at the public library.

It's too dark to go there now.

The poetry class began at the same time the last bell rang at school, so I'd race over there to try and make it without being too late. But even when I was late, everyone seemed happy to have me there—to provide the "feminine teen perspective" they called it.

Looking around, I see that I'm the only one left in Rosie's. They don't close for another thirty minutes. And even though I'm not eating or drinking anymore, the man behind the counter hasn't asked me to leave. So I'll stay.

Imagine ten or twelve orange chairs arranged in a circle, with the happy women from the flyer sitting at opposite ends. Only problem was, from day one, they weren't happy. Someone, whoever made that flyer, must have digitally turned their frowns upside down.

They wrote about death. About the evilness of men. About the destruction of—and I quote—"the greenish, bluish orb with wisps of white."

Seriously, that's how they described it. They went on to call Earth a knocked-up gaseous alien needing an abortion.

Another reason I hate poetry. Who says "orb" instead of "ball" or "sphere?"

"Expose yourself," they said. "Let us see your deepest and your darkest."

My deepest and my darkest? What are you, my gynecologist?

Hannah.

So many times I wanted to raise my hand and say, "Um, so, when do we get to the happy stuff? The stuff about loving life? You know, Poetry: To Love Life? That's what the flyer said. That's why I'm here."

In the end, I only made it through three of those poetry groups. But something did come of it. Something good?

No.

Hmm . . . I wonder.

See, someone else was in that group. Another high schooler with a perspective adored by the older poets. Who was it? The editor of our school's very own Lost-N-Found Gazette.

Ryan Shaver.

You know who I'm talking about. And I'm sure you, Mr. Editor, can't wait for me to say your name out loud.

So here you go, Ryan Shaver. The truth shall set you free.

The motto of the *Lost-N-Found*.

You've known this for a while, Ryan. I'm sure of it. At the first mention of poetry, you knew this one was about you. You had to. Though I'm sure you must have thought, This can't be why I'm on the tapes. It wasn't a big deal.

The poem from school. God, it was hers.

Remember, this is one tight, well-connected, emotional ball I'm constructing here.

I close my eyes tight, covering my eyes with my hand.

I crush my teeth together, jaw muscles burning, to keep from screaming. Or crying. I don't want her to read it. I don't want to hear that poem in her voice.

Would you like to hear the last poem I wrote before quitting poetry? Before quitting poetry for good?

No?

Fine. But you've already read it. It's very popular at our school.

I allow my eyelids, my jaw, to relax.

The poem. We discussed it in English. We read it aloud many times.

And Hannah was there for it all.

Some of you may recall it now. Not word for word, but you know what I'm talking about. The Lost-N-Found Gazette. *Ryan's semiannual collection of items found lying around campus.*

Like a love letter tossed under a desk, never discovered by its intended love. If Ryan found it, he'd scratch out the give-away names and scan it for use in an upcoming gazette.

Photographs that fell out of binders . . . he scanned them, too.

History notes covered in doodles by an extremely bored student . . . he scanned them.

Some people may wonder how Ryan found so many interesting items to scan. Did he really find them at all? Or did he steal them? I asked him that very question after one of our poetry meetings. And he swore that everything he printed was found purely by chance.

Sometimes, he admitted, people did slip items they found into his locker. Those, he said, he couldn't vouch for one hundred percent. That's why he scratched out names and phone numbers. And photographs, as a rule, couldn't be too embarrassing.

He'd gather five or six pages of good, quirky material and print up fifty copies. Then he'd staple them together and drop them off at random places throughout school. Restrooms. Locker rooms. On the track.

"Never in the same spot," he told me. He thought it was fitting for people to stumble across his magazine of stumbled across items.

But guess what? My poem? He stole it.

I pull a napkin out of the holder and wipe the abrasive paper across my eyes.

Each week, after our poetry group, Ryan and I would sit on the library steps and talk. That first week, we simply laughed about the poems the other people had written and read. We laughed about how depressing they all were.

"Wasn't this supposed to make us happy?" he asked. Apparently, he signed up for the same reason as me.

I look up. The man behind the counter tugs on the strings of a heavy trash bag. It's closing time.

"Can I get a glass of water?" I ask.

After the second week of class, we sat on those library steps and read some of our own poems to each other. Poems we'd written at different points in our lives.

He looks at my eyes, at the skin rubbed raw by the napkin.

But only happy poems. Poems about loving life. Poems we would never read to that depression-loving group of miserable poets inside.

And, as poets never do, we explained ourselves. Line for line.

The third week, we took the biggest chance of all and handed each other our entire notebooks of poetry.

He pushes a glass of ice water in front of me. Except for that glass and the napkin dispensers, the entire length of the counter is empty.

Wow! That took a lot of courage. For me, definitely. I'm sure for you, too, Ryan. And for the next two hours, with the sun going down, we sat on those concrete steps, turning pages.

His handwriting was horrible, so it took me a bit longer to read through his poems. But they were amazing. Much deeper than any of mine.

His stuff sounded like real poetry. Professional poetry. And someday, I'm sure of it, kids will be forced to analyze his poems out of a textbook.

I touch the cold glass, wrapping my fingers around it.

Of course, I had no idea what his poems meant. Not exactly. But I felt the emotions precisely. They were absolutely beautiful. And I felt almost ashamed at what he must have been thinking as he went through my notebook. Because reading through his, I realized how little time I'd spent on mine. I should have taken the time to choose better words. More emotional words.

But one of my poems grabbed him. And he wanted to know more about it . . . like when I wrote it.

But I didn't tell him.

I don't drink the water. I watch a single drop slide down the glass and bump against my finger.

I wrote it the same day a group of students got angry that someone had the nerve to ask for help regarding suicide. Remember why they got upset? Because whoever wrote the note didn't sign her name.

How insensitive.

It was anonymous. Just like the poem that appeared in the *Lost-N-Found.*

So Ryan wanted to know why I wrote the poem.

With that one, I told him, the poem had to speak for itself. But I was interested in knowing what he thought it meant.

On the surface, he said, the poem was about acceptance—acceptance from my mother. But more than that, I wanted her approval. And I wanted certain people—in this case a boy—to stop overlooking me.

A boy?

At the base of the glass, the water creates a delicate suction, then lets go. I take a sip and let a small cube of ice slip into my mouth.

I asked if he thought it meant anything deeper.

I hold the ice on my tongue. It's freezing, but I want it to melt there.

Part of me was joking. I thought he'd figured out my poem exactly. But I wanted to know what a teacher assigning the poem might want his or her students to discover. Because teachers always overdo it.

But you found it, Ryan. You found the hidden meaning. You found what even I couldn't find in my own poem.

The poem wasn't about my mom, you said. Or a boy. It was about me. I was writing a letter to myself . . . hidden in a poem.

I flinched when you told me that. I got defensive—even angry. But you were right. And I felt scared, and sad, by my own words.

You told me I wrote that poem because I was afraid of dealing with myself. And I used my mom as an excuse, accusing her of not appreciating or accepting me, when I should have been saying those words into a mirror.

"And the boy?" I asked. "What does he represent?"

It's me. Oh God. It's me. I know that now.

I cover my ears. Not to block any outside noise. The

diner is almost completely silent. But I want to feel her words, all of them, as they're said.

While I waited for your answer, I searched my backpack for tissue. At any moment, I knew I might cry.

You told me that no boy was overlooking me more than I was overlooking myself. At least, that's what you thought it meant. And that's why you asked about the poem. You felt it went deeper than even you could figure out.

Well, Ryan, you were right. It went much, much deeper than that. And if you knew that—if that's what you thought—then why did you steal my notebook? Why did you print my poem, the poem that you yourself called "scary" in the Lost-N-Found*? Why did you let other people read it?*

And dissect it. And make fun of it.

It was never a lost poem, Ryan. And you never found it, so it did not belong in your collection.

But in your collection is exactly where other people found it. That's where teachers stumbled across it right before their lectures on poetry. That's where classrooms full of students cut up my poem, searching for its meaning.

In our class, no one got it right. Not even close. But at the time, we all thought we did. Even Mr. Porter.

Do you know what Mr. Porter said before handing out my poem? He said that reading a poem by an unknown member of our school was the same as reading a classic poem by a dead poet. That's right—a dead poet. Because we couldn't ask either one about its true meaning.

Then Mr. Porter waited, hoping someone would fess up to writing it. But that, as you know, never happened.

So now you know. And for those of you who need a refresher, here it is. "Soul Alone" by Hannah Baker.

I meet your eyes
you don't even see me
You hardly respond
when I whisper
hello
Could be my soul mate
two kindred spirits
Maybe we're not
I guess we'll never
know

My own mother
you carried me in you
Now you see nothing
but what I wear
People ask you
how I am doing
You smile and nod
don't let it end
there

Put me
underneath God's sky and
know me
don't just see me with your eyes
Take away
this mask of flesh and bone and
see me
for my soul

alone

And now you know why.

So, did your teachers dissect me properly? Were they right? Did you have any clue at all it was me?

Yes, some of you did. Ryan must have told someone—proud that his collection made it into the curriculum. But when people confronted me, I refused to confirm it or deny it. Which pissed some of them off.

Some even wrote parodies of my poem, reading them to me in the hopes of getting under my skin.

I saw that. I watched two girls in Mr. Porter's class recite a version before the bell rang.

It was all so stupid and childish . . . and cruel.

They were relentless, bringing new poems every day for an entire week. Hannah did her best to ignore them, pretending to read while waiting for Mr. Porter to arrive. For the start of class to come to her rescue.

This doesn't seem like a big deal, does it?

No, maybe not to you. But school hadn't been a safe haven of mine for a long time. And after your photo escapades, Tyler, my home was no longer secure.

Now, suddenly, even my own thoughts were being offered up for ridicule.

Once, in Mr. Porter's class, when those girls were teasing her, Hannah looked up. Her eyes caught mine for just a moment. A flash. But she knew I was watching her. And even though no one else saw it, I turned away.

She was on her own.

Very nice, Ryan. Thank you. You're a true poet.

■

I pull the headphones out of my ears and hang them around my neck.

"I don't know what's going on with you," the man says from across the counter, "but I'm not taking your money." He blows into a straw and pinches both ends shut.

I shake my head and reach back for my wallet. "No, I'll pay."

He winds the straw tighter and tighter. "I'm serious. It was only a milkshake. And like I said, I don't know what's going on, and I don't know how I can help, but something's clearly gone wrong in your life, so I want you to keep your money." His eyes search mine, and I know he means it.

I don't know what to say. Even if the words would come, my throat is so tight it won't let them escape.

So I nod, grab my backpack, and change the tape as I head for the door.

CASSETTE 5: SIDE A

The glass door to Rosie's closes behind me, and I hear three locks immediately slide into place.

So now where? Home? Back to Monet's? Or maybe I'll go to the library after all. I can sit outside on the concrete steps. Listen to the remainder of the tapes in the dark.

"Clay!"

It's Tony's voice.

Bright headlights flash three times. The driver's-side window is down and Tony's outstretched hand waves me over. I tug the zipper on my jacket up and walk over to his window. But I don't lean in. I don't feel like talking. Not now.

Tony and I have known each other for years, working on projects and joking around after class. And all that time, we've never had a deep conversation.

Now, I'm afraid, he wants to have one. He's been sitting here this whole time. Just sitting in his car. Waiting. What else could be on his mind?

He won't look at me. Instead, he reaches out to adjust the side mirror with his thumb. Then he closes his eyes and lets his head fall forward. "Get in, Clay."

"Is everything all right?"

After a short pause, slowly, he nods.

I walk around the front of his car, open the passenger door, and sit, keeping one foot out on the blacktop. I place my backpack, with Hannah's shoebox inside it, on my lap.

"Shut the door," he says.

"Where are we going?"

"It's okay, Clay. Just shut the door." He winds the handle on his door and his window slides up. "It's cold outside." His gaze slips from the dashboard to the stereo to his steering wheel. But he won't face me.

The moment I pull the door shut, like the trigger on a starting pistol, he begins.

"You're the ninth person I've had to follow, Clay."

"What? What are you talking about?"

"The second set of tapes," he says. "Hannah wasn't bluffing. I've got them."

"Oh, God." I cover my face with both hands. Behind my eyebrow, the pounding is back again. With the base of my palm, I press on it. Hard.

"It's okay," he says.

I can't look at him. What does he know? About me? What has he heard? "What's okay?"

"What were you listening to in there?"

"What?"

"Which tape?"

I can try and deny it, pretend I have no clue what he's talking about. Or I can get out of his car and leave. But either way, he knows.

"It's okay, Clay. Honest. Which tape?"

With my eyes still shut, I press my knuckles against my forehead. "Ryan's," I say. "The poem." Then I look at him.

He leans his head back, eyes closed.

"What?" I ask.

No answer.

"Why'd she give them to you?"

He touches the key-chain dangling in the ignition. "Can I drive while you listen to the next tape?"

"Tell me why she gave them to you."

"I'll tell you," he says, "if you'll just listen to the next tape right now."

"Why?"

"Clay, I'm not joking. Listen to the tape."

"Then answer my question."

"Because it's about you, Clay." He lets go of his keys. "The next tape is about you."

Nothing.

My heart doesn't jump. My eyes don't flinch. I don't breathe.

And then.

I snap my arm back, my elbow into the seat. Then I smash it into the door and I want to pound my head sideways into the window. But I pound it back against the headrest instead.

Tony lays a hand on my shoulder. "Listen to it," he says. "And don't leave this car."

He turns the ignition.

With tears falling, I roll my head to face him. But he's staring straight ahead.

I open the door of the Walkman and pull out the tape. The fifth tape. A dark blue number nine in the corner. My tape. I am number nine.

I drop the tape back into the Walkman and, holding the player in both hands, close it like a book.

Tony puts the car in gear and drives through the empty parking lot, heading for the street.

Without looking, I run my thumb across the top of the Walkman, feeling for the button that brings me into the story.

▶

Romeo, oh Romeo. Wherefore art thou, Romeo?

My story. My tape. This is how it begins.

Good question, Juliet. And I wish I knew the answer.

Tony shouts over the engine. "Clay, it's okay!"

To be totally honest, there was never a point where I said to myself, Clay Jensen . . . he's the one.

Just hearing my name, the pain in my head doubles. I feel an agonizing twist in my heart.

I'm not even sure how much of the real Clay Jensen I got to know over the years. Most of what I knew was secondhand information. And that's why I wanted to know him better. Because everything I heard—and I mean everything!—was good.

It was one of those things where, once I noticed it, I couldn't stop noticing it.

Kristen Rennert, for example. She always wears black. Black pants. Or black shoes. Black shirt. If it's a black jacket, and that's the only black she's wearing, she won't take it off all day. The next time you see her, you'll notice it. And then you won't be able to stop noticing it.

Steve Oliver's the same way. Whenever he raises his hand to say something, or ask a question, he always begins with the words "all right."

"Mr. Oliver?"

"All right, if Thomas Jefferson was a slave owner . . . "

"Mr. Oliver?"

"All right, I got 76.1225."

"Mr. Oliver?"

"All right, can I have a hall pass?"

Seriously. Every time. And now you'll notice it, too . . . every time.

Yes, I've noticed it, Hannah. But let's get on with it. Please.

Overhearing gossip about Clay became a similar distraction. And like I said, I didn't know him very well, but my ears perked up whenever I heard his name. I guess I wanted to hear something—anything—juicy. Not because I wanted to spread gossip. I just couldn't believe someone could be that good.

I glance at Tony and roll my eyes. But he's driving, looking straight ahead.

If he actually was that good . . . wonderful. Great! But it became a personal game of mine. How long could I go on hearing nothing but good things about Clay Jensen?

Normally, when a person has a stellar image, another person's waiting in the wings to tear them apart. They're waiting for that one fatal flaw to expose itself.

But not with Clay.

Again, I look over at Tony. This time, he's smirking.

I hope this tape doesn't make you run out and dig for that deep, dark, and dirty secret of his . . . which I'm sure is there. At least one or two of them, right?

I've got a few.

But wait, isn't that what you're doing, Hannah? You're setting him up as Mr. Perfect only to tear him down. You,

Hannah Baker, were the one waiting in the wings. Waiting for a flaw. And you found it. And now you can't wait to tell everyone what it is and ruin his image.

To which I say . . . no.

My chest relaxes, freeing a breath of air I didn't even know I was holding.

And I hope you're not disappointed. I hope you aren't just listening—salivating—for gossip. I hope these tapes mean more to you than that.

Clay, honey, your name does not belong on this list.

I lean my head against the window and close my eyes, concentrating on the cold glass. Maybe if I listen to the words but concentrate on the cold, maybe I can hold it together.

You don't belong in the same way as the others. It's like that song: One of these things is not like the others. One of these things just doesn't belong.

And that's you, Clay. But you need to be here if I'm going to tell my story. To tell it more completely.

II

"Why do I have to hear this?" I ask. "Why didn't she just skip me if I don't belong?"

Tony keeps driving. If he looks anywhere other than straight ahead, it's only briefly into the rearview mirror.

"I would've been happier never hearing this," I say.

Tony shakes his head. "No. It would drive you crazy not knowing what happened to her."

I stare through the windshield at the white lines glowing in the headlights. And I realize he's right.

"Besides," he says, "I think she wanted you to know."

Maybe, I think. But why? "Where are we going?"

He doesn't answer.

▶

Yes, there are some major gaps in my story. Some parts I just couldn't figure out how to tell. Or couldn't bring myself to say out loud. Events I haven't come to grips with . . . that I'll never come to grips with. And if I never have to say them out loud, then I never have to think them all the way through.

But does that diminish any of your stories? Are your stories any less meaningful because I'm not telling you everything?

No.

Actually, it magnifies them.

You don't know what went on in the rest of my life. At home. Even at school. You don't know what goes on in anyone's life but your own. And when you mess with one part of a person's life, you're not messing with just that part. Unfortunately, you can't be that precise and selective. When you mess with one part of a person's life, you're messing with their entire life.

Everything . . . affects everything.

The next few stories are centered around one night.

The party.

They're centered around our night, Clay. And you know what I mean by our night because, through all the years we've spent going to the same school or working together at the movie theater, there's only one night when we connected.

when we really connected.

That night as well drags many of you into the story . . . one of you for the second time. A random night that none of you can take back.

I hated that night. Even before these tapes, I hated it. That night, I ran to tell an old woman that her husband was fine. Everything was going to be fine. But I was lying. Because while I was running to comfort his wife, the other driver was dying.

And the old man, by the time he got home to his wife, he knew it.

Hopefully, no one will hear these tapes except for those of you on this list, leaving any changes they bring to your lives completely up to you.

Of course, if the tapes do get out, you'll have to deal with consequences completely out of your control. So I sincerely hope you're passing them on.

I glance at Tony. Would he really do that? Could he? Would he give the tapes to someone not on the list?

Who?

For some of you, those consequences may be minimal. Maybe shame. Or embarrassment. But for others, it's hard to say. A lost job? Jail time?

Let's keep this between us, shall we?

So Clay, I wasn't even supposed to be at that party. I was invited, but I wasn't supposed to be there. My grades were slipping pretty fast. My parents asked for progress reports every week from my teachers. And when none of them came back with improvements, I was grounded.

For me, grounded meant that I had one hour to get home from school. One hour being my only free time until I brought those grades up.

We're at a stoplight. And still, Tony keeps his eyes straight ahead. Does he want to avoid seeing me cry? Because he doesn't have to worry, I'm not. Not right now.

During one of my Clay Jensen gossip moments, I found out that you were going to be at the party.

What? Clay Jensen at a party? Unheard of.

I study on the weekends. In most of my classes, we're tested every Monday. It's not my fault.

Not only was that my first thought, that's what the people around me were talking about, too. No one could figure out why they never saw you at parties. Of course, they had all sorts of theories. But guess what? That's right. None of them were bad.

Give me a break.

As you know, since Tyler's not tall enough to peep through a second-story window, sneaking out of my bedroom wasn't hard to do. And that night, I just had *to do it. But don't jump to conclusions. I've snuck out of my house, before that night, only twice.*

Okay, three times. Maybe four. Tops.

For those of you who don't know which party I'm talking about, there's a red star on your map. A big, fat, red star completely filled in. C-6. Five-twelve Cottonwood.

Is that where we're going?

Aaaah . . . so now you know. Now some of you know exactly where you fit in. But you'll have to wait until your name pops up to hear what I'm going to tell. To hear how much I tell.

That night, I decided that walking to the party would be nice. Relaxing. We had a lot of rain that week, and I remember the clouds were still hanging low and thick. The air was warm for that time of night, too. My absolute favorite type of weather.

Mine, too.

Pure magic.

It's funny. Walking by the houses on my way to the party, it felt like life held so many possibilities. Limitless possibilities. And for the first time in a long time, I felt hope.

So did I. I forced myself out of the house and to that

party. I was ready for something new to happen. Something exciting.

Hope? Well, I guess I misread things a bit.

And now? Knowing what happened between Hannah and me, would I still have gone? Even if nothing changed?

It was simply the calm before the storm.

I would. Yes. Even if the outcome stayed the same.

I wore a black skirt with a matching hooded pullover. And on my way there, I took a three-block detour to my old house—the one I lived in when we first moved to town. The first red star from the first side of the first tape. The porch light was on and, in the garage, a car's engine was running.

But the garage door was shut.

Am I the only one who knows this? Does anyone else know that's where he lived? The man from the accident. The man who's car killed a student from our school.

I stopped walking and, for what seemed like several minutes, just watched from the sidewalk. Mesmerized. Another family in my house. I had no idea who they were or what they were like—what their lives were like.

The garage door began to lift and, in the glow of the red taillights, the silhouette of a man pushed the heavy door all the way up. He got in the car, backed it down the driveway, and drove off.

Why he didn't stop, why he didn't ask why I was standing there staring at his house, I don't know. Maybe he thought I was waiting for him to back out of the driveway before continuing on my merry way.

But whatever the reason, it felt surreal. Two people—me and him—one house. Yet he drove away with no idea of his link to me, the girl on the sidewalk. And for some reason, at that moment, the air felt heavy. Filled with loneliness. And that loneliness stayed with me through the rest of the night.

Even the best moments of the night were affected by that one incident—by that nonincident—in front of my old house. His lack of interest in me was a reminder. Even though I had a history in that house, it didn't matter. You can't go back to how things were. How you thought they were.

All you really have . . . is now.

Those of us on the tapes, we can't go back, either. We can never *not* find a package on our doorstep. Or in our mailbox. From that moment on, we're different.

Which explains my overreaction, Clay. And that's why you'll get these tapes. To explain. To say I'm sorry.

Does she remember? Does she remember that I apologized to her that night? Is that why she's apologizing to me?

The party was well underway by the time I got there. Most people, unlike me, didn't have to wait for their parents to fall asleep.

The usual crowd hung out by the front door of the party, drunk out of their minds, greeting everyone with a raised cup of beer. I would think Hannah would be a hard name to slur, but those guys did it pretty well. Half of them kept repeating my name, trying to get it right, while the other half laughed.

But they were harmless. Fun drunks make a nice addition to any party. Not looking to fight. Not looking to score. Just looking to get drunk and laugh.

I remember those guys. Like the mascots of the party. "Clay! Whatchoo doon here? Bah-ha-ha-ha!"

The music was loud and no one was dancing. It could have been any party . . . except for one thing.

Clay Jensen.

I'm sure you heard a lot of sarcastic remarks when you first arrived, but by the time I got there, to everyone else you were just a part of the party. But unlike everyone else, you were the whole reason I came.

With everything going on in my life—going on in my head—I wanted to talk with you. Really talk. Just once. A chance we never seemed to get at school. Or at work. A chance to ask, Who are you?

We didn't get that chance because I was afraid. Afraid I had no chance with you.

That's what I thought. And I was fine with that. Because what if I got to know you and you turned out to be just like they said? What if you weren't the person I hoped you were?

That, more than anything, would have hurt the most.

And as I stood in the kitchen, in line to fill my cup for the first time, you walked up behind me.

"Hannah Baker," you said, and I turned toward you. "Hannah . . . hey."

When she first arrived, when she walked through the front door, she caught me off guard. And like a freak, I turned around, ran through the kitchen, and straight out the back.

It was too soon, I told myself. I went to the party telling myself that if Hannah Baker showed up, I was going to talk to her. It was time. I didn't care who was there, I was going to keep my eyes focused on her and we were going to talk.

But then she walked in and I freaked out.

I couldn't believe it. Out of the blue, there you were.

No, not out of the blue. First I paced around the backyard, cursing myself for being such a scared little boy. Then I let myself out through the gate, fully intent on walking home.

But on the sidewalk, I beat myself up some more. Then I walked back to the front door. The drunk people greeted me again, and I went straight for you.

It was anything but out of the blue.

"I don't know why," you said, "but I think we need to talk."

It took all the guts in the world to keep that conversation going. Guts and two plastic cups of beer.

And I agreed, with probably the dumbest smile plastered on my face.

No. The most beautiful.

And then I noticed the doorframe behind you, leading into the kitchen. It had a bunch of pen and pencil marks scratched on it, keeping track of how fast the children in the house were growing. And I remembered watching my mom erase those marks on our old kitchen door, getting ready to sell the house to move here.

I saw that. I saw something in your eyes when you looked over my shoulder.

Anyway, you looked at my empty cup, poured half of your drink into mine, and asked if now would be a good time to talk.

Please don't read into that, people. Yes, it sounds all smooth and get-the-girl-drunk, but it wasn't. It didn't seem that way to me.

It wasn't. No one's going to buy that, but it's true.

Because if that was the case, he would have encouraged me to fill my cup all the way.

So we walked into the living room, where one side of the couch was occupied.

By Jessica Davis and Justin Foley.

But there was plenty of room on the other end, so we sat down. And what was the first thing we did? We set down our cups and started talking. Just . . . like . . . that.

She had to know it was them. Jessica and Justin. But she didn't say their names. The first boy she kissed kissing the girl who slapped her at Monet's. It was like she couldn't escape her past.

Everything I could have hoped for was happening. The questions were personal, as if catching up for the time we let pass. Yet the questions never felt intrusive.

Her voice, if physically possible, comes through the headphones feeling warm. I place cupped hands over my ears to keep her words from escaping.

And they weren't intrusive. Because I wanted you to know me.

It was wonderful. I couldn't believe Hannah and I were finally talking. Really talking. And I did not want it to stop.

I loved talking with you, Hannah.

It seemed like you could know me. Like you could understand anything I told you. And the more we spoke, I knew why. The same things excited us. The same things concerned us.

You could have told me anything, Hannah. That night, nothing was off limits. I would've stayed till you opened up and let everything out, but you didn't.

I wanted to tell you everything. And that hurt because some things were too scary. Some things even I didn't understand. How could I tell someone—someone I was really talking to for the first time—everything I was thinking?

I couldn't. It was too soon.

But it wasn't.

Or maybe it was too late.

But you're telling me now. Why did you wait till now?

Her words, they're not warm anymore. She might want me to hear them that way, but they're burning me up instead. In my mind. In my heart.

Clay, you kept saying that you knew things would flow easily between us. You felt that way for a long time, you said. You knew we'd get along. That we would connect.

But how? You never explained that. How could you know? Because I knew what people said about me. I heard all the rumors and lies that will always be a part of me.

I knew they weren't true, Hannah. I mean, I hoped they weren't true. But I was too afraid to find out.

I was breaking. If only I'd talked to you sooner. We could have been . . . we could've . . . I don't know. But things had gone too far by then. My mind was set. Not on ending my life. Not yet. It was set on floating through school. On never being close to anyone. That was my plan. I'd graduate, then I'd leave.

But then, I went to a party. I went to a party to meet you.

Why did I do that? To make myself suffer? Because that's what I was doing—hating myself for waiting so long. Hating myself because it wasn't fair to you.

The only thing that's not fair are these tapes, Hannah,

because I was there for you. We were talking. You could have said anything. I would have listened to absolutely anything.

The couple sitting beside us on the couch, the girl was drunk and laughing and bumping into me every so often. Which was funny at first, but it got old real fast.

Why isn't Hannah saying her name?

I started to think maybe she wasn't so drunk after all. Maybe it was all a show for the guy she was talking with . . . when they were actually talking. Maybe she wanted the couch all to herself and her guy.

So Clay and I left.

We walked around the party, shouting over the music wherever we went. Eventually—successfully—I spun the conversation around. No more big and heavy topics. We needed to laugh. But everywhere we went it was too noisy to hear each other.

So we wound up in the doorway to an empty room.

I remember everything that happened next. I remember it perfectly. But how does she remember it?

While we were standing there, our backs against the doorframe, drinks in hand, we couldn't stop laughing.

And yet the loneliness I entered the party with came rushing back.

But I wasn't alone. I knew that. For the first time in a long time, I was connecting—connected—with another person from school. How in the world was I alone?

You weren't. Hannah, I was there.

Because I wanted to be. That's all I can say. It's all that makes sense to me. How many times had I let myself connect with someone only to have it thrown back in my face?

Everything seemed good, but I knew it had the potential to be awful. Much, much more painful than the others.

There was no way that was going to happen.

So there you were, letting me connect with you. And when I couldn't do that anymore, when I pulled the conversation to lighter topics, you made me laugh. And you were hilarious, Clay. You were exactly what I needed.

So I kissed you.

No, I kissed you, Hannah.

A long and beautiful kiss.

And what did you say when we came up for air? With the cutest, littlest, boyish smirk, you asked, "What was that for?"

Right. You kissed me.

To which I said, "You're such an idiot." And we kissed some more.

An idiot. Yes, I remember that, too.

Eventually we shut the door and moved deeper into the room. We were on one side of the door. And the rest of the party, with its loud but muffled music, was on the other.

Amazing. We were together. That's what I kept thinking the whole time. Amazing. I had to concentrate so hard to keep that word from spilling out of my mouth.

Some of you may be wondering, How come we never heard about this? We always found out who Hannah made out with.

Because I never told.

Wrong. You only thought you found out. Haven't you been listening? Or did you only pay attention to the tape with your name on it? Because I can count on one hand—yes, one hand—how many people I've made out with. But you, you probably thought I'd need both hands and both feet just to get started, right?

What's that? You don't believe me? You're shocked? Guess what . . . I don't care. The last time I cared what anyone thought about me was that night. And that was the last night.

I unbuckle my seatbelt and lean forward. I clasp my hand over my mouth and squeeze to keep from screaming.

But I do scream, the sound dampened in the palm of my hand.

And Tony keeps driving.

Now get comfortable, because I'm about to tell you what happened in that room between Clay and me. Are you ready?

We kissed.

That's it. We kissed.

I look down at my lap, at the Walkman. It's too dark to see the spindles behind the plastic window, pulling the tape from one side to the other, but I need to focus on something, so I try. And concentrating on the spot where the two spindles should be is the closest I get to looking into Hannah's eyes as she tells my story.

It was wonderful, both of us lying on the bed. One of his hands resting on my hip. His other arm cradling my head like a pillow. Both of my arms hugging him, trying to pull him closer. And speaking for myself, I wanted more.

That's when I said it. That's when I whispered to her, "I'm so sorry." Because inside, I felt so happy and sad at the same time. Sad that it took me so long to get there. But happy that we got there together.

The kisses felt like first kisses. Kisses that said I could start over if I wanted to. With him.

But start over from what?

And that's when I thought of you, Justin. For the first time in a long time, I thought of our first kiss. My real first kiss. I remembered the anticipation leading up to it. I remembered your lips pressed against mine.

And then I remembered how you ruined it.

"Stop," I told Clay. And my hands stopped pulling him in.

You pushed your hands against my chest.

Could you feel what I was going through, Clay? Did you sense it? You must have.

No. You hid it. You never told me what it was, Hannah.

I shut my eyes so tight it was painful. Trying to push away all that I was seeing in my head. And what I saw was everyone on this list . . . and more. Everyone up to that night. Everyone who caused me to be so intrigued by Clay's reputation—how his reputation was so different from mine.

No, we were the same.

And I couldn't help that. What everyone thought of me was out of my control.

Clay, your reputation was deserved. But mine . . . mine was not. And there I was, with you. Adding to my reputation.

But it wasn't like that. Who was I going to tell, Hannah?

"Stop," I repeated. This time I moved my hands under your chest and pushed you away. I turned to the side, burying my face in the pillow.

You started to talk, but I made you stop. I asked you to leave. You started to talk again and I screamed. I screamed into the pillow.

And then you stopped talking. You heard me.

The bed lifted on your side as you got up to leave the room. But it took you forever to leave, to realize that I was serious.

I was hoping you'd tell me to stop again. To stop leaving.

Even though my eyes remained shut, buried in the pillow, the light changed when you finally opened the door. It grew brighter. Then it faded again . . . and you were gone.

Why did I listen? Why did I leave her there? She needed me and I knew that.

But I was scared. Once again, I let myself get scared.

And then I slid off the bed and down to the floor. I just sat there beside the bed, hugging my knees . . . and crying.

That, Clay, is where your story ends.

But it shouldn't have. I was there for you, Hannah. You could have reached out but you didn't. You chose this. You had a choice and you pushed me away. I would have helped you. I wanted to help you.

You left the room and we never spoke again.

Your mind was set. No matter what you say, it was set.

In the hallways at school, you tried catching my eye, but I always looked away. Because that night, when I got home, I tore a page from my notebook and wrote down one name after another after another. The names in my head when I stopped kissing you.

There were so many names, Clay. Three dozen, at least.

And then . . . I made the connections.

I circled your name first, Justin. And I drew a line from you to Alex. I circled Alex and drew a line to Jessica, bypassing names that didn't connect—that just floated there—incidents all by themselves.

My anger and frustration with all of you turned to tears and then back to anger and hate every time I found a new connection.

And then I reached Clay, the reason I went to the party. I circled his name and drew a line . . . back. Back to a previous name.

It was Justin.

In fact, Clay, soon after you left and shut the door . . . that person reopened it.

On Justin's tape, the first tape, she said his name would reappear. And he was at that party. On the couch with Jessica.

But that person's already received the tapes. So Clay, just skip him when you pass them on. In a roundabout way, he caused a new name to be added to this list. And that's who should receive the tapes from you.

And yes, Clay—I'm sorry, too.

■

My eyes sting. Not from the salt in my tears, but because I haven't closed them since learning Hannah cried when I left the room.

Every muscle in my neck burns to turn away. To look out the window, away from the Walkman, and let my eyes stare into nothing. But I can't bring myself to move, to break the effect of her words.

Tony slows the car and pulls over to a curb. "You okay?"

It's a residential street, but it's not the street of the party.

I shake my head no.

"Are you going to be okay?" he asks.

I lean back, resting my head against the seat, and close my eyes. "I miss her."

"I miss her, too," he says. And when I open my eyes, his head is down. Is he crying? Or maybe trying not to cry.

"The thing is," I say, "I never really missed her till now."

He sits back in his seat and looks over at me.

"I didn't know what to make of that night. Everything that happened. I'd liked her for so long from far away, but I never had a chance to tell her." I look down at the Walkman. "We only had one night, and by the end of that night, it seemed like I knew her even less than before. But now I know. I know where her mind was that night. Now I know what she was going through."

My voice breaks, and in that break comes a flood of tears.

Tony doesn't respond. He looks out into the empty street, allowing me to sit in his car and just miss her. To miss her each time I pull in a breath of air. To miss her with a heart that feels so cold by itself, but warm when thoughts of her flow through me.

I wipe the cuff of my jacket under my eyes. Then I choke back my tears and laugh. "Thanks for listening to all that," I say. "Next time, it's okay to stop me."

Tony turns on the blinker, looks over his shoulder, and pulls us back into the street. But he doesn't look at me. "You're welcome."

CASSETTE 5: SIDE B

It feels like we've driven this same road multiple times since leaving Rosie's. Like he's stalling for time.

"Were you at the party?" I ask.

Tony looks out his side window and changes lanes. "No. Clay, I need to know that you're going to be all right."

Impossible to answer. Because no, I didn't push her away. I didn't add to her pain or do anything to hurt her. Instead, I left her alone in that room. The only person who might've been able to reach out and save her from herself. To pull her back from wherever she was heading.

I did what she asked and I left. When I should have stayed.

"No one blames me," I whisper. I need to hear it said

aloud. I need to hear the words in my ears and not just in my head. "No one blames me."

"No one," Tony says, his eyes still on the road.

"What about you?" I ask.

We approach a four-way stop and slow down.

For a moment, from the corner of his eye, he looks at me. Then he returns his gaze to the road. "No, I don't blame you."

"But why you?" I ask. "Why did she give you the other set of tapes?"

"Let me drive you to the party house," he says. "I'll tell you there."

"You can't tell me now?"

His smile is weak. "I'm trying to keep us on the road."

▶

Soon after Clay left, the couple from the couch walked into the bedroom. Actually, stumbled into the bedroom is more accurate. Remember them? I thought she was acting drunk, bumping into me so we'd get up and leave. Unfortunately, it wasn't an act. She was smashed.

I passed them in the hall. One of Jessica's arms lay flopped over Justin's shoulders. The other one groped for the wall to steady herself.

Of course, I didn't actually see them come in. I was still on the floor, my back against the far side of the bed, and it was dark.

When I walked out of the room, I felt so frustrated. So confused. I leaned against the piano in the living room, almost needing it to hold myself up. What should I do? Stay? Leave? But where would I go?

Her sofa buddy kept her from stumbling too hard into the nightstand. And when she rolled off the bed . . . twice . . . he lifted her back on. Nice guy that he was, he kept the laughter to a minimum.

I thought he would tuck her in and shut the door behind him as he left. And that would be the perfect time for my getaway. End of story.

Hannah wasn't my first kiss, but the first kiss that mattered; the first kiss with someone who mattered. And after talking with her for so long that night, I assumed it was just the beginning. Something was happening between us. Something right. I felt it.

But that's not the end of the story. Because that wouldn't make for a very interesting tape, now would it? And by now, I'm sure you knew it wasn't the end.

Still, with no destination in mind, I left the party.

Instead of leaving, he started kissing her.

I know, some of you would have easily stayed for such an amazing voyeuristic opportunity. A close encounter of the sexual kind. Even if you never saw it, at least you'd hear it.

But two things kept me down on that floor. With my forehead pressed against my knees, I realized how much I must've drank that night. And with my balance not what it should've been, to run across the floor felt a little hazardous.

So that's one excuse.

Excuse number two is that things seemed to be winding down up there. Not only was she drunk and clumsy, she seemed to be completely unresponsive. From what I could tell, it didn't go much beyond kissing. And it seemed to be one-sided kissing at that.

Again, nice guy that he was, he didn't take advantage of the situation. He wanted to. He tried for the longest time to get a reaction out of her. "Are you still awake? Do you want me to take you to the bathroom? Are you gonna puke?"

This girl wasn't totally passed out. She grunted and groaned a bit.

It dawned on him—finally—that she wasn't in a romantic mood and probably wouldn't be for a while. So he tucked her in and said he'd check on her in a bit. Then he left.

At this point you might be wondering, Who are these people? Hannah, you forgot to tell us their names. But I didn't forget. If there's one thing I've still got, it's my memory.

Which is too bad. Maybe if I forgot things once in a while, we'd all be a little bit happier.

The mist was heavy when I left the party. And as I walked through the neighborhood, it started to drizzle.

Then rain. But when I first started walking it was just a thick mist that left everything sort of hazy.

No, you'll have to wait for a name on this one. Though if you've been paying close attention, I gave you the answer a long time ago.

Before I say his name out loud, this guy needs to stew a bit . . . to remember everything that happened in that room.

And he remembers. I know he does.

I would love to see his face right now. His eyes shut tight. Jaw clenched. Fists pulling out his hair.

And to him I say, Deny it! Go on, deny that I was ever in that room. Deny that I know what you did. Or not what you did, but what you didn't do. What you allowed to happen. Rationalize why this isn't the tape you're making a return appearance on. It must be a later tape. It has to be a later tape.

Oh, really? And you'd like that? A later tape would make things better?

Don't bet on it.

God. What else could've gone wrong that night?

I know she wasn't your girlfriend, that you hardly ever talked to her and barely even knew her, but is that your best excuse for what happened next? Or is that your only excuse?

Either way, there is no excuse.

I stood up, stabilizing myself with one hand on the bed.

Your shoes—the shadow of your shoes—were still visible

in the light coming under the door. Because when you left that room, you took up post right outside. And I let go of the bed and started walking toward that sliver of light, not sure what I'd say to you when I opened the door.

But halfway there, two more shoes came into view . . . and I stopped.

When I left the party, I just walked. Several blocks. Not wanting to go home. Not wanting to go back.

The door opened, but you pulled it back and said, "No. Let her rest."

In that tiny burst of light, I saw a closet—its accordion doors halfway open. Meanwhile, your friend was convincing you to let him in that room.

I waited, heart pounding, trapped in the middle of the floor.

The bedroom door opened again. But again, you pulled it shut. And you tried to make a joke of it. "Trust me," you said, "she won't move. She'll just lay there."

And what was his response? What was it? What was his reasoning for you to step aside and let him in that room? Do you remember? Because I do.

It was the night shift.

He told you he was working the night shift and had to leave in a few minutes.

A few minutes, that's all he needed with her. So just relax and step aside.

And that's all it took for you to let him open the door.

God.

Pathetic.

I couldn't believe it. And your friend couldn't believe it, either, because when he grabbed the doorknob again, he didn't rush right in. He waited for you to protest.

In that brief moment—the moment you said nothing—I fell on my knees, sick, covering my mouth with both hands. I stumbled toward the closet, tears blurring the light from the hall. And when I collapsed into the closet, a pile of jackets on the floor caught me.

When the bedroom door opened, I pulled the closet doors shut. And I shut my eyes tight. Blood pounded in my ears. I rocked back and forth, back and forth, beating my forehead into the pile of jackets. But with the bass pumping throughout the house, no one heard me.

"Just relax." Those words, he's said it before. It's what he always says to the people he's taking advantage of. Girlfriends. Guys. Whoever.

It's Bryce. It has to be. Bryce Walker was in that room.

And with the bass thumping, no one heard him walking across the room. Walking across the room. Getting on the bed. The bedsprings screaming under his weight. No one heard a thing.

And I could have stopped it. If I could have talked. If I could have seen. If I could have thought about anything, I would have opened those doors and stopped it.

But I didn't. And it doesn't matter what my excuse was. That my mind was in a meltdown is no excuse. I have no excuse. I could have stopped it—end of story. But to stop it, I felt like I'd have to stop the entire world from spinning. Like things had been out of control for so long that whatever I did hardly mattered anymore.

And I couldn't stand all the emotions anymore. I wanted the world to stop . . . to end.

For Hannah, the world did end. But for Jessica, it didn't. It went on. And then, Hannah hit her with these tapes.

I don't know how many songs went by with my face buried in those jackets. The beats kept sliding from one song into another. After a while, my throat felt so scratched. So raw and burning. Had I been screaming?

With my knees on the floor, I felt vibrations whenever anyone walked down the hall. And when footsteps fell within the room—several songs after he entered the room—I pressed my back against the closet wall . . . waiting. Waiting for the closet doors to be torn open. To be yanked out of my hiding place.

And then? What would he do to me then?

Tony's car pulls over. The front tire scrapes the curb. I don't know how we got here, but the house is right outside my window now. The same front door where I entered the party. The same front porch where I left. And to the left of the porch, a window. Behind that window, a bedroom and a closet with accordion doors where Hannah, on the night I kissed her, disappeared.

But light from the hallway seeped into the room, into the closet, and his footsteps walked away. It was over.

After all, he couldn't be late for work, could he?

So what happened next? Well, I ran out of the room and straight down the hall. And that's where I saw you. Sitting in a room all by yourself. The person this whole tape revolves around . . . Justin Foley.

My stomach lurches and I fling open the car door.

Sitting on the edge of a bed, with the lights turned off, there you were.

Sitting there, staring at nothing. While I stood in the hallway, frozen, staring at you.

We'd come a long way, Justin. From the first time I watched you slip on Kat's lawn. To my first kiss at the bottom of the slide. To now.

First, you started a chain of events that ruined my life. Now, you were working on hers.

Outside that very same house, I throw up.

I keep my body hunched over, my head hanging over the gutter.

Eventually, you turned my way. The color in your face . . . gone. Your expression . . . blank. And your eyes looked so exhausted.

Or was it pain I saw there?

"Stay there as long as you want," Tony says.

Don't worry, I think. I won't puke in your car.

Justin, baby, I'm not blaming you entirely. We're in this one together. We both could have stopped it. Either one of us. We could have saved her. And I'm admitting this to you. To all of you. That girl had two chances. And both of us let her down.

The breeze feels good on my face, cooling the sweat on my forehead and neck.

So why is this tape about Justin? What about the other guy? Isn't what he did worse?

Yes. Absolutely yes. But the tapes need to be passed on. And if I sent them to him, they would stop. Think about it. He raped a girl and would leave town in a second if he knew . . . well . . . if he knew that we knew.

II

Still hunched over, I breathe in as fully as possible. Then I hold it.

And release.

Breathe. Then hold.

Release.

I sit upright in the seat, keeping the door open just in case. "Why you?" I ask. "Why do you have these tapes? What did you do?"

A car drives by and we both watch it turn left two blocks

away. It's another minute before Tony answers.

"Nothing," he says. "And that's the truth." For the first time since approaching me at Rosie's, Tony addresses me eye to eye. And in his eyes, catching the light from a lamppost half a block away, I see tears. "Finish this tape, Clay, and I'll explain everything."

I don't answer.

"Finish it. You're almost done," he says.

So what do you think of him now, Justin? Do you hate him? Your friend that raped her, is he still your friend?

Yes, but why?

It must be denial. It has to be. Sure, he's always had a temper. Sure, he goes through girls like used underwear. But he's always been a good friend to you. And the more you hang out with him, the more he seems like the same old guy from before, right? And if he acts like the same guy, then he couldn't possibly have done anything wrong. Which means that you didn't do anything wrong, either.

Great! That's great news, Justin. Because if he didn't do anything wrong, and you didn't do anything wrong, then I didn't do anything wrong. And you have no idea how much I wish I didn't ruin that girl's life.

But I did.

At the very least, I helped. And so did you.

No, you're right, you didn't rape her. And I didn't rape her. He did. But you . . . and I . . . we let it happen.

It's our fault.

■

"Full story," I say. "What happened?"

I pull the sixth tape from my pocket and swap it with the one inside the Walkman.

CASSETTE 6: SIDE A

Tony takes his keys out of the ignition. Something to hold on to while he talks. "I've been trying to figure out how to say this the whole time we've been driving. The whole time we've been sitting here. Even when you were puking your guts out."

"You noticed I didn't puke in your car."

"I did." He smiles, looking down at his keys. "Thanks. I appreciate that."

I close the car door. My stomach is settling.

"She came over to my house," Tony says. "Hannah. And that was my chance."

"For what?"

"Clay, the signs were all there," he says.

"I had my chance, too," I tell him. I take off the headphones and hang them on my knee. "At the party. She was freaking out when we kissed and I didn't know why. That was my chance."

Inside the car, it's dark. And quiet. With the windows rolled up the outside world seems deep asleep.

"We're all to blame," he says. "At least a little."

"So she came over to your house," I say.

"With her bike. The one she always rode to school."

"The blue one," I say. "Let me guess. You were working on your car."

He laughs. "Who would've thought, right? But she never came over to my house before, so I was a little surprised. You know, we were friendly at school, so I didn't think too much of it. What was weird, though, was why she came over."

"Why?"

He looks out the side window, and his chest fills with air. "She came over to give me her bike."

The words sit there, undisturbed, for an uncomfortably long time.

"She wanted me to have it," he says. "She was done with it. When I asked for a reason, she just shrugged. She didn't have one. But it was a sign. And I missed it."

I summarize a bullet point from the handout at school. "Giving away possessions."

Tony nods. "She said I was the only one she could think

of who might need it. I drive the oldest car at school, she said, and she thought if it ever broke down I might need a backup."

"But this baby never breaks down," I say.

"This thing always breaks down," he says. "I'm just always around to fix it. So I told her that I couldn't take her bike. Not without giving her something in return."

"What did you give her?"

"I'll never forget this," he says, and he turns to look at me. "Her eyes, Clay, they never looked away. She just kept looking, straight into my eyes, and started crying. She just stared at me and tears began streaming down her face."

He wipes away tears from his own eyes and then wipes a hand across his upper lip. "I should have done something."

The signs were all there, all over, for anyone willing to notice.

"What did she ask for?"

"She asked me how I made my tapes, the ones I play in my car." He leans his head back and takes a deep breath. "So I told her about my dad's old tape recorder." He pauses. "Then she asked if I had anything to record voices."

"God."

"Like a handheld recorder or something. Something you didn't have to plug in but could walk around with. And I didn't ask why. I told her to wait right there and I'd get one."

"And you gave it to her?"

He turns to me, his face hard. "I didn't know what she was going to do with it, Clay."

"Wait, I'm not accusing you, Tony. But she didn't say anything about why she wanted it?"

"If I had asked, do you think she would have told me?"

No. By the time she went to Tony's house, her mind was made up. If she wanted someone to stop her, to rescue her from herself, I was there. At the party. And she knew it.

I shake my head. "She wouldn't have told you."

"A few days later," he says, "when I get home from school, there's a package sitting on my porch. I take it up to my room and start listening to the tapes. But it doesn't make any sense."

"Did she leave you a note or anything?"

"No. Just the tapes. But it didn't make any sense because Hannah and I have third period together and she was at school that day."

"What?"

"So when I got home and started listening to the tapes, I went through them so fast. Fast-forwarding to find out if I was on them. But I wasn't. And that's when I knew that she'd given me the second set of tapes. So I looked her up and called her house, but no one answered. So I called her parents' store. I asked if Hannah was there, and they asked if everything was all right because I'm sure I sounded crazy."

"What did you say?"

"I told them that something was wrong and they needed to find her. But I couldn't make myself tell them why." He takes in a thin, jagged breath of air. "And the next day at school, she wasn't there."

I want to tell him I'm sorry, that I can't imagine what that must've been like. But then I think of tomorrow, at school, and realize I'll find out soon enough. Seeing the other people on the tapes for the first time.

"I went home early that day," he says, "pretending I was sick. And I've got to admit, it took me a few days to pull myself together. But when I returned, Justin Foley looked like hell. Then Alex. And I thought, okay, most of these people deserve it, so I'm going to do what she asked and make sure you all hear what she has to say."

"But how are you keeping track?" I ask. "How did you know I had the tapes?"

"You were easy," he says. "You stole my Walkman, Clay."

We both laugh. And it feels good. A release. Like laughing at a funeral. Maybe inappropriate, but definitely needed.

"But everyone else, they were a little trickier," he says. "I'd run to my car after the last bell and drive as close to the front lawn of the school as possible. When I saw whoever was next, a couple days after I knew the last person had heard the tapes, I'd call out his name and wave him over. Or her. I'd wave her over."

"And then you'd just ask if they had the tapes?"

"No. They would've denied it, right? So I'd hold up a tape when they got close and tell them to get in because I had a song I wanted them to hear. Every time, based on their reaction, I knew."

"And then you'd play one of her tapes?"

"No. If they didn't run away, I'd have to do something, so I'd play them a song," he says. "Any song. They would sit there, where you are, wondering why in the hell I was playing them this song. But if I was right, their eyes would glaze over, like they were a million miles away."

"So why you?" I ask. "Why'd she give the tapes to you?"

"I don't know," he says. "The only thing I can think of is because I gave her the recorder. She thought I had a stake in it and would play along."

"You're not on them, but you're still a part."

He faces the windshield and grips the steering wheel. "I've got to go."

"I didn't mean anything by that," I say. "Honest."

"I know. But it's late. My dad's going to start wondering if I broke down somewhere."

"What, you don't want him messing under your hood again?" I grab the door handle and then, remembering, let go and pull out my phone. "I need you to do something. Can you say hello to my mom?"

"Sure."

I scroll through the list of names, hit Send, and she picks up right away.

"Clay?"

"Hey, Mom."

"Clay, where are you?" She sounds hurt.

"I told you I might be out late."

"I know. You did. I was just hoping to hear from you by now."

"I'm sorry. But I'm going to need a little longer. I may need to stay at Tony's tonight."

Right on cue, "Hello, Mrs. Jensen."

She asks if I've been drinking.

"Mom, no. I swear."

"Okay, well, this is for his history project, right?"

I flinch. She wants to believe my excuses so bad. Every time I lie, she wants to believe me so much.

"I trust you, Clay."

I tell her I'll be home before school to get my stuff, then we hang up.

"Where are you going to stay?" Tony asks.

"I don't know. I'll probably go home. But I don't want her to worry if I don't."

He turns the key, the engine starts, and he flips on the headlights. "Do you want me to take you somewhere?"

I grab the door handle and nod toward the house. "This is where I'm at in the tapes," I say. "But thanks."

His eyes stare straight ahead.

"Honestly. Thank you," I say. And when I say it, I mean it for more than just the ride. For everything. For how he reacted when I broke down and cried. For trying to make me laugh on the most horrible night of my life.

It feels good knowing someone understands what I'm listening to, what I'm going through. Somehow, it makes it not as scary to keep listening.

I get out of the car and shut the door. His car pulls away.

I press Play.

▶

Back to the party, everyone. But don't get too comfy, we'll be leaving in just a minute.

Half a block away, Tony's Mustang stops at an intersection, takes a left, and drives away.

If time was a string connecting all of your stories, that party would be the point where everything knots up. And that knot keeps growing and growing, getting more and more tangled, dragging the rest of your stories into it.

When Justin and I finally broke that awful, painful stare, I wandered down the hall and back into the party. Staggered in, really. But not from the alcohol. From everything else.

I sit on the curb, a few feet from where I vomited out of Tony's car. If whoever lives here, because I have no idea whose party it was, wants to come out and ask me to leave, I welcome it. Please do.

I grabbed for the piano in the living room. Then the piano bench. And I sat.

I wanted to leave, but where would I go? I couldn't go home. Not yet.

And wherever I went, how would I get there? I was too weak to walk. At least, I thought I was too weak. But in truth, I was too weak to try. The only thing I knew for certain was that I wanted to get out of there and not think about anything or anyone anymore.

Then a hand touched my shoulder. A gentle squeeze.

It was Jenny Kurtz.

The cheerleader from the Student Body office.

Jenny, this one's for you.

I drop my head down to my knees.

Jenny asked if I needed a ride home, and I almost laughed. Was it so obvious? Did I look that terrible?

So I looped my arm in hers and she helped me up. Which felt good, letting someone help me. We walked out the front door, through a crowd either passed out on the porch or smoking in the yard.

Somewhere, at that moment, I was walking from block to block trying to figure out why I'd left that party. Trying to figure out, trying to understand, what had just happened between me and Hannah.

The sidewalk was damp. My feet, numb and heavy, shuf-

fled across the pavement. I listened to the sound of every pebble and leaf that I stepped on. I wanted to hear them all. To block out the music and the voices behind me.

While blocks away, I could still hear that music. Distant. Muffled. Like I couldn't get far enough away.

And I can still remember every song that played.

Jenny, you didn't say a thing. You didn't ask me any questions. And I was so grateful. Maybe you've had things happen, or seen things happen at parties that you just couldn't discuss. Not right away, at least. Which is sort of fitting, because I haven't discussed any of this until now.

Well . . . no . . . I tried. I tried once, but he didn't want to hear it.

Is that the twelfth story? The thirteenth? Or something else entirely? Is it one of the names written on her paper that she won't tell us about?

So, Jenny, you led me to your car. And even though my thoughts were somewhere else—my eyes focused on nothing—I felt your touch. You held my arm with such tenderness as you lowered me into the passenger seat. You buckled me in, got in your seat, then we left.

What happened next, I'm not entirely sure. I wasn't paying attention because, in your car, I felt secure. The air inside was warm and comforting. The wiper blades, on a slow speed, gently pulled me out of my thoughts and into the car. Into reality.

The rain wasn't heavy, but it blurred the windshield just

enough to keep everything dreamlike. And I needed that. It kept my world from becoming too real, too fast.

And then . . . it hit. There's nothing like an accident to bring the world crashing back.

An accident? Another one? Two in one night? How come I never heard about this one?

The front wheel on my side slammed into and jumped the curb. A wooden post smacked into your front bumper and snapped back like a toothpick.

God. No.

A Stop sign fell backward in front of your headlights. It caught under your car and you screamed and slammed on the brakes. In the side mirror, I watched sparks fly onto the road as we slid to a stop.

Okay, now I'm awake.

We sat for a moment, staring through the windshield. No words, not a glance between us. The wipers smeared the rain from side to side. And my hands stayed gripped to my seatbelt, thankful we only hit a sign.

The accident with the old man. And the guy from school. Did Hannah know? Did she know Jenny caused it?

Your door opened and I watched you walk to the front of your car, then crouch between the headlights for a closer look. You ran a hand over the dent and let your head droop forward. I couldn't tell if you were pissed. Or were you crying?

Maybe you were laughing at how horrible the night was turning out.

I know where to go. I don't need the map. I know exactly where the next star is, so I stand up to start walking.

The dent wasn't bad. I mean, it wasn't good, but you had to feel some relief. It could have been worse. It could have been much, much worse. For example . . . you could have hit something else.

She knows.

Something alive.

Whatever your initial thoughts, you stood up with a blank expression. Just standing there, staring at the dent, shaking your head.

Then you caught my eye. And I'm sure I saw a frown, even if it lasted only a split second. But that frown turned into a smile. Followed by a shrug.

And what were the first words you said when you got back in the car? "Well, that sucks." Then you put your key in the ignition and . . . I stopped you. I couldn't let you drive away.

At the intersection where Tony turned left, I take a right. It's still two blocks away, but I know it's there. The Stop sign.

You shut your eyes and said, "Hannah, I'm not drunk."

Well, I didn't accuse you of being drunk, Jenny. But I was wondering why the hell you couldn't keep your car on the road.

"It's raining," you said.

And yes, true, it was. Barely.

I told you to park the car.

You told me to be reasonable. We both lived close by and you'd stick to the residential streets—as if that made it any better.

I see it. A metal pole holding up a Stop sign, its reflective letters visible even this far away. But on the night of the accident, it was a different sign. The letters weren't reflective and the sign had been fastened to a wooden post.

"Hannah, don't worry," you said. Then you laughed. "Nobody obeys Stop signs anyway. They just roll on through. So now, because there isn't one there, it's legal. See? People will thank me."

Again, I told you to park the car. We'd get a ride home from someone at the party. I'd pick you up first thing in the morning and drive you to your car.

But you tried again. "Hannah, listen."

"Park it," I said. "Please."

And then you told me to get out. But I wouldn't. I tried reasoning with you. You were lucky it was only a sign. Imagine what could happen if I let you drive us all the way home.

But again, "Get out."

I sat for a long time with my eyes shut, listening to the rain and the wipers.

"Hannah! Get . . . out!"

So finally, I did. I opened the car door and stepped out. But I didn't shut it. I looked back at you. And you stared through your windshield—through the wipers—gripping the wheel.

Still a block away, but the only thing I can focus on is the Stop sign straight ahead.

I asked if I could use your phone. I saw it sitting there right below the stereo.

"Why?" you asked.

I'm not sure why I told you the truth. I should have lied. "We need to at least tell someone about the sign," I said.

You kept your eyes straight ahead. "They'll trace it. They can trace phone calls, Hannah." Then you started up the car and told me to shut the door.

I didn't.

So you reversed the car, and I jumped back to keep the door from knocking me over.

You didn't care that the metal sign was crushing—grating—the underside of your car. When you cleared it, the sign lay at my feet, warped and streaked with silver scratches.

You revved the engine and I took the hint, stepping back onto the curb. Then you peeled away, causing the door to slam shut, picking up speed the further you got . . . and you got away.

In fact, you got away with much more than knocking down a sign, Jenny.

And once again, I could have stopped it . . . somehow.

We all could have stopped it. We all could have stopped something. The rumors. The rape.

You.

There must have been something I could have said. At the very least, I could have taken your keys. Or at the very, very least, I could have reached in and stolen your phone to call the police.

Actually, that's the only thing that would've mattered. Because you found your way home in once piece, Jenny. But that wasn't the problem. The sign was knocked down, and that was the problem.

B-6 on your map. Two blocks from the party there's a Stop sign. But on that night, for part of the night, there wasn't. And it was raining. And someone was trying to deliver his pizzas on time. And someone else, headed in the opposite direction, was turning.

The old man.

There was no Stop sign on that corner. Not on that night. And one of them, one of the drivers, died.

No one knew who caused it. Not us. Not the police.

But Jenny knew. And Hannah. And maybe Jenny's parents, because someone fixed her bumper real fast.

I never knew the guy in that car. He was a senior. And

when I saw his picture in the newspaper, I didn't recognize him. Just one of the many faces at school I never got to know . . . and never would.

I didn't go to his funeral, either. Yes, maybe I should have, but I didn't. I couldn't. And now I'm sure it's obvious why.

She didn't know. Not about the man in the other car. She didn't know it was the man from her house. Her old house. And I'm glad. Earlier, she watched him pull out of his garage. She watched him drive away without noticing her.

But some of you were there, at his funeral.

Driving to return a toothbrush. That's what his wife told me as we waited on her couch for the police to bring him home. He was driving to the other end of town to return their granddaughter's toothbrush. They'd been keeping an eye on her while her parents were on vacation, and she'd left it behind by accident. The girl's parents said there was no need to drive across town just for that. They had plenty of extras. "But that's what he does," his wife told me. "That's the kind of person he is."

And then the police came.

For those of you who did go, let me describe what school was like on the day of his funeral. In a word . . . it was quiet. About a quarter of the school took the morning off. Mostly seniors, of course. But for those of us who did go to school, the teachers let us know that if we simply forgot to bring a note from home, they wouldn't mark us absent if we wanted to attended the funeral.

Mr. Porter said funerals can be a part of the healing process. But I doubted that very much. Not for me. Because on that corner, there wasn't a Stop sign that night. Someone had knocked it over. And someone else . . . yours truly . . . could've stopped it.

Two officers helped her husband inside, his body trembling. His wife got up and walked over to him. She wrapped him in her arms and they cried.

When I left, closing the door behind me, the last thing I saw was the two of them standing in the middle of the living room. Holding each other.

On the day of the funeral, so those of you who attended wouldn't miss any work, the rest of us did nothing. In every class, the teachers gave us free time. Free to write. Free to read.

Free to think.

And what did I do? For the first time, I thought about my own funeral.

More and more, in very general terms, I'd been thinking about my own death. Just the fact of dying. But on that day, with all of you at a funeral, I began thinking of my own.

I reach the Stop sign. With the tips of my fingers, I reach forward and touch the cold metal pole.

I could picture life—school and everything else—continuing on without me. But I could not picture my funeral. Not at all. Mostly because I couldn't imagine who would attend or what they would say.

I had . . . I have . . . no idea what you think of me.

I don't know what people think of you either, Hannah. When we found out, and since your parents didn't have a funeral in this town, no one said much about it at all.

I mean, it was there. We felt it. Your empty desk. The fact that you would not be coming back. But no one knew where to begin. No one knew how to start that conversation.

It's now been a couple of weeks since the party. So far, Jenny, you've done a great job of hiding from me. I suppose that's understandable. You'd like to forget what we did—what happened with your car and the Stop sign. The repercussions.

But you never will.

Maybe you didn't know what people thought of you because they themselves didn't know what they thought of you. Maybe you didn't give us enough to go on, Hannah.

If not for that party, I never would have met the real you. But for some reason, and I am extremely grateful, you gave me that chance. However brief it was, you gave me a chance. And I liked the Hannah I met that night. Maybe I could've even loved her.

But you decided not to let that happen, Hannah. It was you who decided.

I, on the other hand, only have to think about it for one more day.

I turn away from the Stop sign and walk away.

If I had known two cars were going to crash on that corner, I would've run back to the party and called the cops immediately. But I never imagined that would happen. Never.

So instead, I walked. But not back to the party. My mind was racing all over the place. I couldn't think straight. I couldn't walk straight.

I want to look back. To look over my shoulder and see the Stop sign with huge reflective letters, pleading with Hannah. Stop!

But I keep facing forward, refusing to see it as more than it is. It's a sign. A stop sign on a street corner. Nothing more.

I turned corner after corner with no idea where I was going.

We walked those streets together, Hannah. Different routes, but at the same time. On the same night. We walked the streets to get away. Me, from you. And you, from the party. But not just from the party. From yourself.

And then I heard tires squeal, and I turned, and I watched two cars collide.

Eventually, I made it to a gas station. C-7 on your map. And I used a payphone to call the police. As it rang, I found myself hugging the receiver, part of me hoping that no one would answer.

I wanted to wait. I wanted the phone to just keep ringing. I wanted life to stay right there . . . on pause.

I can't follow her map anymore. I am not going to the gas station.

When someone finally did answer, I sucked in the tears that wet my lips and told them that on the corner of Tanglewood and South . . .

But she cut me off. She told me to calm down. And that's when I realized how hard I had been crying. How much I was struggling to catch one good breath.

I cross the street and move further away from the party house.

Over the past few weeks, I've walked out of my way so many times to avoid that house. To avoid the reminder, the pain, of my one night with Hannah Baker. I have no desire to see it twice in one night.

She told me the cops had already been called and were on their way.

I swing my backpack in front of me and pull out the map.

I was shocked. I couldn't believe you actually called the police, Jenny.

I unfold the map to give it one last look.

But I shouldn't have been shocked. Because as it turns out, you didn't call them.

Then I crumple it up, crushing the map into a ball the size of my fist.

At school the next day, when everyone replayed the events of what happened the previous night, that's when I found out who had called. And it wasn't to report a fallen sign.

I stuff the map deep into a bush and walk away.

It was to report an accident. An accident caused by a fallen sign. An accident I was never aware of . . . until then.

But that night, after hanging up the phone, I wandered the streets some more. Because I had to stop crying. Before I went home, I needed to calm down. If my parents caught me sneaking back in with tears in my eyes, they'd ask way too many questions. Unanswerable questions.

That's what I'm doing now. Staying away. I wasn't crying the night of the party, but I can barely hold it back now.

And I can't go home.

So I walked without thinking about which roads to take. And it felt good. The cold. The mist. That's what the rain had turned into by then. A light mist.

And I walked for hours, imagining the mist growing thick and swallowing me whole. The thought of disappearing like that—so simply—made me so happy.

But that, as you know, never happened.

■

I pop open the Walkman to flip the tape. I'm almost at the end.

God. I let out a quivering breath and close my eyes. The end.

CASSETTE 6: SIDE B

▶

Just two more to go. Don't give up on me now.

I'm sorry. I guess that's an odd thing to say. Because isn't that what I'm doing? Giving up?

Yes. As a matter of fact, I am. And that, more than anything else, is what this all comes down to. Me . . . giving up . . . on me.

No matter what I've said so far, no matter who I've spoken of, it all comes back to—it all ends with—me.

Her voice sounds calm. Content with what she's saying.

Before that party, I'd thought about giving up so many times. I don't know, maybe some people are just preconditioned to think about it more than others. Because every time something bad happened, I thought about it.

It? Okay, I'll say it. I thought about suicide.

The anger, the blame, it's all gone. Her mind is made up. The word is not a struggle for her anymore.

After everything I've talked about on these tapes, everything that occurred, I thought about suicide. Usually, it was just a passing thought.

I wish I would die.

I've thought those words many times. But it's a hard thing to say out loud. It's even scarier to feel you might mean it.

But sometimes I took things further and wondered how I would do it. I would tuck myself into bed and wonder if there was anything in the house I could use.

A gun? No. We never owned one. And I wouldn't know where to get one.

What about hanging? Well, what would I use? Where would I do it? And even if I knew what and where, I could never get beyond the visual of someone finding me—swinging—inches from the floor.

I couldn't do that to Mom and Dad.

So how did they find you? I've heard so many rumors.

It became a sick sort of game, imagining ways to kill myself. And there are some pretty weird and creative ways.

You took pills. That, we all know. Some say you passed out and drowned in a bathtub full of water.

It came down to two lines of thinking. If I wanted people

to think it was an accident, I'd drive my car off the road. Someplace where there's no chance of survival. And there are so many places to do that on the outskirts of town. I've probably driven by each of them a dozen times in the past couple weeks.

Others say you drew the bathwater, but fell asleep on your bed while it was filling. Your mom and dad came home, found the bathroom flooded, and called your name. But there was no answer.

Then there are these tapes.

Can I trust the twelve of you to keep a secret? To not let my parents find out what really happened? Will you let them believe it was an accident if that's the story going around?

She pauses.

I don't know. I'm not sure.

She thinks we might tell. She thinks we'll walk up to our friends and say, "Do you want to know a horrible secret?"

So I've decided on the least painful way possible.

Pills.

My stomach pulls in, wanting to rid my body of everything. Food. Thoughts. Emotions.

But what kind of pills? And how many? I'm not sure. And I don't have much time to figure it out because tomorrow . . . I'm going to do it.

Wow.

I sit down on the curb of a dark, quiet intersection.

I won't be around anymore . . . tomorrow.

Most houses on the connecting four blocks give little indication that anyone is awake inside. A few windows flicker with the faint blue light of late-night TV. About a third of them have porch lights on. But for the rest, other than a cut lawn or a car out front, it's hard to tell anyone lives there at all.

Tomorrow I'm getting up, I'm getting dressed, and I'm walking to the post office. There, I'll mail a bunch of tapes to Justin Foley. And after that, there's no turning back. I'll go to school, too late for first period, and we'll have one last day together. The only difference being that I'll know it's the last day.

You won't.

Can I remember? Can I see her in the halls on that last day? I want to remember the very last time I saw her.

And you'll treat me how you've always treated me. Do you remember the last thing you said to me?

I don't.

The last thing you did to me?

I smiled, I'm sure of it. I smiled every time I saw you after that party, but you never looked up. Because your mind was made up.

If given the chance, you knew you might smile back. And you couldn't. Not if you wanted to go through with it.

And what was the last thing I said to you? Because trust me, when I said it, I knew it was the last thing I'd ever say.

Nothing. You told me to leave the room and that was it. You found ways to ignore me every time after that.

Which brings us to one of my very last weekends. The weekend following the accident. The weekend of a new party. A party I didn't attend.

Yes, I was still grounded. But that's not the reason I didn't go. In fact, if I wanted to go, it would've been much easier than last time because I was house-sitting that weekend. A friend of my father's was out of town and I was watching his house for him, feeding his dog, and keeping an eye on things because there was supposed to be a rager a few doors down.

And there was. Maybe not as big as the last party, but definitely not one for beginners.

Even if I thought you might be there, I still would've stayed home.

With the way you ignored me at school, I assumed you would ignore me there, too. And that was a theory too painful to prove.

I've heard people say that after a particularly bad experience with tequila, just the smell of it can make them barf. And while this party didn't make me barf, just being near it—just hearing it—twisted my stomach into knots.

One week was nowhere near enough time to get over that last party.

The dog was going crazy, yapping every time someone walked by the window. I would crouch down, yelling at him to get away from there, but was too afraid to go over and pick him up—too afraid someone might see me and call my name.

So I put the dog in the garage, where he could yap all he wanted.

Wait, I remember it now. The last time I saw you.

The bass thumping down the block was impossible to shut out. But I tried. I ran through the house, closing curtains and twisting shut every blind I could find.

I remember the last words we said to each other.

Then I hid myself in the bedroom with the TV blasting. And even though I couldn't hear it, I could feel the bass pumping inside of me.

I shut my eyes, tight. I wasn't watching the TV anymore. I wasn't in that room anymore. I could only think back to that closet, hiding inside it with a pile of jackets surrounding me. And once again, I started rocking back and forth, back and forth. And once again, no one was around to hear me cry.

In Mr. Porter's English class, I noticed your desk was empty. But when the bell rang and I walked into the hall, there you were.

Eventually the party died down. And after everyone walked by the window again, and the dog stopped yapping,

I walked through the house reopening the curtains.

We almost bumped into each other. But your eyes were down so you didn't know it was me. And together, we said it. "I'm sorry."

After being shut in for so long, I decided to catch a breath of fresh air. And maybe, in turn, be a hero.

Then you looked up. You saw me. And there, in your eyes, what was it? Sadness? Pain? You moved around me and tried pushing your hair away from your face. Your fingernails were painted dark blue. I watched you walk down the long stretch of hallway, with people knocking into me. But I didn't care.

I stood there and watched you disappear. Forever.

Once again, everybody, D-4. Courtney Crimsen's house. The site of this party.

No, this tape is not about Courtney . . . though she does play a part. But Courtney has no idea what I'm about to say because she left just as things got going.

I turn and walk in the opposite direction of Courtney's house.

My plan was to just walk by the place. Maybe I'd find someone struggling to put a key in their car door and I'd give them a ride home.

I'm not going to Courtney's. I'm going to Eisenhower Park, the scene of Hannah's first kiss.

But the street was empty. Everyone was gone.

Or so it seemed.

And then, someone called my name.

Over the tall wooden fence at the side of her house, a head poked up. And whose head would that be? Bryce Walker's.

God, no. This can only end one way. If anyone can shovel more shit onto Hannah's life, it's Bryce.

"Where you going?" he asked.

How many times had I seen him, with any of his girlfriends, grabbing their wrists and twisting? Treating them like meat.

And that was in public.

My body, my shoulders, everything was set to keep walking by the house. And I should have kept walking. But my face turned toward him. There was steam rising up from his side of the fence.

"Come on, join us," he said. "We're sobering up."

And whose head should pop up beside his? Miss Courtney Crimsen's.

Now there was a coincidence. She's the one who used me as a chauffer to attend a party. And there I was, crashing her after-party.

She's the one who left me stranded with no one to talk to. And there I was, at her house, where she had nowhere to hide.

That's not why you did it, Hannah. That's not why you

joined them. You knew it was the worst choice possible. You knew that.

But who am I to hold a grudge?

That's why you did it. You wanted your world to collapse around you. You wanted everything to get as dark as possible. And Bryce, you knew, could help you do that.

He said you were all just relaxing a bit. Then you, Courtney, offered to give me a ride home when we were done, not realizing "home" was only two houses away. And you sounded so genuine, which surprised me.

It even made me feel a little guilty.

I was willing to forgive you, Courtney. I do forgive you. In fact, I forgive almost all of you. But you still need to hear me out. You still need to know.

I walked across the wet grass and pulled a latch on the fence, popping the gate open a few inches. And behind it, the source of the steam . . . a redwood hot tub.

The jets weren't on, so the only sound was the water lapping against the sides. Against the two of you.

Your heads were back, resting on the edge of the hot tub. Your eyes were shut. And the little smiles on your faces made the water and steam look so inviting.

Courtney rolled her head my way but kept her eyes shut. "We're in our underwear," she said.

I waited a second. Should I?

No . . . but I will.

You knew what you were getting into, Hannah.

I took off my top, pulled off my shoes, took off my pants, and climbed the wooden steps. And then? I descended into the water.

It felt so relaxing. So comforting.

I cupped the hot water in my hands and let it drip over my face. I pushed it back through my hair. I forced my eyes to shut, my body to slide down, and my head to rest against the ledge.

But with the calming water also came terror. I should not be here. I didn't trust Courtney. I didn't trust Bryce. No matter what their original intentions, I knew them each well enough not to trust them for long.

And I was right not to trust them . . . but I was done. I was through fighting. I opened my eyes and looked up at the night sky. Through the steam, the whole world seemed like a dream.

I narrow my eyes as I walk, wanting to shut them completely.

Before long, the water became uncomfortable. Too hot.

When I open my eyes, I want to be standing in front of the park. I don't want to see any more of the streets I walked, and the streets Hannah walked, the night of the party.

But when I pushed my back against the tub and sat up to cool my upper body, I could see my breasts through my wet bra.

So I slid back down.

And Bryce slid over . . . slowly . . . across the underwater bench. And his shoulder rested against mine.

Courtney opened her eyes, looked at us, then shut them again.

I swing a fist to the side and rattle a rusted chain-link fence. I shut my eyes and drag my fingers across the metal.

Bryce's words were soft, an obvious attempt at romance. "Hannah Baker," he said.

Everyone knows who you are, Bryce. Everyone knows what you do. But I, for the record, did nothing to stop you.

You asked if I had fun at the party. Courtney whispered that I wasn't at the party, but you didn't seem to care. Instead, your fingertips touched the outside of my thigh.

I open my eyes and pound the fence again.

I clenched my jaw and your fingers moved away.

"It broke up pretty fast," you said. And just as fast, your fingertips were back.

I hold tight to the fence and keep walking forward. When my fingers pull away from the metal, my skin slices open.

Your whole hand was back. And when I didn't stop you, you slid your hand across my belly. Your thumb touched the bottom of my bra and your pinky touched the top of my underwear.

I turned my head sideways, away from you. And I know I didn't smile.

You pulled your fingers together and rubbed slow, full circles around my stomach. "Feels nice," you said.

I felt a shift in the water and opened my eyes for one brief second.

Courtney was walking away.

Do you need more reasons for everyone to hate you, Courtney?

"Remember when you were a freshman?" you asked.

Your fingers made their way under my bra. But you didn't grab me. Testing the boundaries, I guess. Sliding your thumb along the underside of my breasts.

"Weren't you on that list?" you said. "Best ass in the freshman class."

Bryce, you had to see my jaw clench. You had to see my tears. Does that kind of shit turn you on?

Bryce? Yes. It does.

"It's true," you said.

And then, just like that, I let go. My shoulders went limp. My legs fell apart. I knew exactly what I was doing.

Not once had I given in to the reputation you'd all set for me. Not once. Even though sometimes it was hard. Even though, sometimes, I found myself attracted to someone who only wanted to get with me because of what they'd heard. But I always said no to those people. Always!

Until Bryce.

So congratulations, Bryce. You're the one. I let my reputation catch up with me—I let my reputation become me—with you. How does it feel?

Wait, don't answer that. Let me say this first: I was not attracted to you, Bryce. Ever. In fact, you disgusted me.

And I'm going to kick your ass. I swear it.

You were touching me . . . but I was using you. I needed you, so I could let go of me, completely.

For everyone listening, let me be clear. I did not say no or push his hand away. All I did was turn my head, clench my teeth, and fight back tears. And he saw that. He even told me to relax.

"Just relax," he said. "Everything will be okay." As if letting him finger me was going to cure all my problems.

But in the end, I never told you to get away . . . and you didn't.

You stopped rubbing circles on my stomach. Instead, you rubbed back and forth, gently, along my waist. Your pinky made its way under the top of my panties and rolled back and forth, from hip to hip. Then another finger slipped below, pushing your pinky further down, brushing it through my hair.

And that's all you needed, Bryce. You started kissing my shoulder, my neck, sliding your fingers in and out. And then you kept going. You didn't stop there.

I'm sorry. Is this getting too graphic for some of you? Too bad.

When you were done, Bryce, I got out of the hot tub and walked two houses away. The night was over.

I was done.

■

I tighten my fist and lift it in front of my face. Through my teary eyes, I watch the blood squeeze through my fingers. The skin is cut deep in a few places, torn by the rusted fence.

No matter where Hannah wants me to go next, I know where I'm spending the rest of my night. But first, I need to clean my hand. The cuts sting, but I mostly feel weak from the sight of my own blood.

I head for the nearest gas station. It's a couple of blocks down and not too far out of my way. I flick my hand a few times, dripping dark spots of blood onto the sidewalk.

When I reach the station, I tuck my hurt hand into my pocket and pull open the glass door of the mini-mart. I find a clear bottle of rubbing alcohol and a small box of Band-Aids, drop a few bucks on the counter, and ask for a key to the restroom.

"Restrooms are around back," the woman behind the counter says.

I turn the key in the lock and push the restroom door open with my shoulder. Then I rinse my hand beneath cold water and watch the blood circle down the drain. I crack the seal on the bottle of alcohol and, in one motion because I won't do it if I think, empty the entire bottle over my hand.

My whole body tenses and I curse as loud and as hard as I can. It feels like my skin is peeling away from the muscle.

After what seems like nearly an hour, I can finally bend and flex my fingers again. Using my free hand and my teeth, I apply some Band-Aids to my cut hand.

I return the key and the woman says nothing more than, "Have a good night."

When I reach the sidewalk, I start jogging again. There's only one tape left. A blue number thirteen painted in the corner.

CASSETTE 7: SIDE A

Eisenhower Park is empty. I stand silently at the entrance, taking it all in. This is where I'll spend the night. Where I'll listen to the last words Hannah Baker wants to say before I let myself fall asleep.

Lampposts stand in the various play areas, but most of the bulbs are either burnt out or busted. The bottom half of the rocket slide is hidden in darkness. But near the top, where the rocket climbs higher than the swings and the trees, moonlight hits the metal bars all the way up to the peak.

I step onto an area of sand surrounding the rocket. I duck beneath its bottom platform, lifted up from the ground by three large metal fins. Above me, a circle the size of a manhole is cut into the lowest level. A metal ladder descends to the sand.

When I stand up, my shoulders poke through the hole. With my good hand, I grip the lip of the circle and climb to the first platform.

I reach into my jacket pocket and press Play.

▶

One . . . last . . . try.

She's whispering. The recorder is close to her mouth and with each break in her words I can hear her breathe.

I'm giving life one more chance. And this time, I'm getting help. I'm asking for help because I cannot do this alone. I've tried that.

You didn't, Hannah. I was there for you and you told me to leave.

Of course, if you're listening to this, I failed. Or he failed. And if he fails, the deal is sealed.

My throat tightens, and I start climbing up the next ladder.

Only one person stands between you and this collection of audiotapes: Mr. Porter.

No! He cannot know about this.

Hannah and I both have Mr. Porter for first-period English. I see him every day. I do not want him to know about this. Not about me. Not about anyone. To bring an adult into this, someone from school, is beyond what I imagined.

Mr. Porter, let's see how you do.

The sound of Velcro tearing apart. Then stuffing. She's

shoving the recorder into something. A backpack? Her jacket?

She knocks.

And knocks again.

—Hannah. Glad you made it.

The voice is muffled, but it's him. Deep, but friendly.

—Come in. Sit here.

Thank you.

Our English teacher, but also the guidance counselor for students with last names *A* through *G*. Hannah Baker's guidance counselor.

—Are you comfortable? Do you want some water?

I'm fine. Thank you.

—So, Hannah, how can I help you? What would you like to talk about?

Well, that's . . . I don't know, really. Just everything, I guess.

—That might take a while.

A long pause. Too long.

—Hannah, it's okay. I've got as much time as you need. Whenever you're ready.

It's just . . . things. Everything's so hard right now.

Her voice is shaky.

I don't know where to begin. I mean, I kind of do. But there's so much and I don't know how to sum it all up.

—You don't need to sum it all up. Why don't we begin with how you're feeling today.

Right now?

—Right now.

Right now I feel lost, I guess. Sort of empty.

—Empty how?

Just empty. Just nothing. I don't care anymore.

—About?

Make her tell you. Keep asking questions, but make her tell you.

About anything. School. Myself. The people in my school.

—What about your friends?

You're going to have to define "friends" if you want an answer to that question.

—Don't tell me you don't have friends, Hannah. I see you in the halls.

Seriously, I need a definition. How do you know what a friend is?

—Someone you can turn to when . . .

Then I don't have any. That's why I'm here, isn't it? I'm turning to you.

—Yes. You are. And I'm glad you're here, Hannah.

I crawl across the second platform and kneel beside an opening in the bars. An opening big enough for people to crawl through to reach the slide.

You don't know how hard it was to set up this meeting.

—My schedule's been fairly open this week.

Not hard to schedule. Hard to get myself here.

Moonlight catches the smooth metal of the slide. I can imagine Hannah here, about two years ago, pushing off and sliding down.

Slipping away.

—Again, I'm glad that you're here, Hannah. So tell me, when you leave this office, how do you want things to be different for you?

You mean, how can you help?

—Yes.

I guess I . . . I don't know. I'm not sure what I'm expecting.

—Well, what do you need right now that you're not getting? Let's start there.

I need it to stop.

—You need what to stop?

I need everything to stop. People. Life.

I push myself back from the slide.

—Hannah, do you know what you just said?

She knows what she said, Mr. Porter. She wants you to notice what she said and help her.

—You said you wanted life to stop, Hannah. Your life?

No response.

—Is that what you meant to say, Hannah? Those are very serious words, you know.

She knows every word that comes out of her mouth, Mr. Porter. She knows they're serious words. Do something!

I know. They are. I'm sorry.

Don't apologize. Talk to him!

I don't want my life to end. That's why I'm here.

—So what happened, Hannah? How did we get here?

We? Or how did I *get here?*

—You, Hannah. How did you get to this point? I know you can't sum it all up. It's the snowball effect, am I right?

Yes. The snowball effect. That's what she's been calling it.

—It's one thing on top of another. It's too much, isn't it?

It's too hard.

—Life?

Another pause.

I grab onto the outer bars of the rocket and pull myself up. My bandaged hand hurts. It stings to put my weight on it, but I don't care.

—Here. Take this. An entire box of tissues just for you. Never been used.

A laugh. He got her to laugh!

Thank you.

—Let's talk about school, Hannah. So I can get some idea how we—I'm sorry—how you got to this point.

Okay.

I start climbing to the top level.

—When you think of school, what's the first thing that comes to mind?

Learning, I guess.

—Well, that's good to hear.

I'm kidding.

Now Mr. Porter laughs.

I do learn here, but that's not what school is for me.

—Then what is it for you?

A place. Just a place filled with people that I'm required to be with.

I sit on the top platform.

—And that's hard for you?

At times.

—With certain people, or people in general?

With certain people. But also . . . everyone.

—Can you be a little more specific?

I scoot backward across the platform and lean against the metal steering wheel. Above the tree line, the half-moon is almost too bright to look at.

It's hard because I don't know who's going to . . . you know . . . get me next. Or how.

—What do you mean, "get" you?

Not like a conspiracy or anything. But it feels like I never know when something's going to pop out of the woodwork.

—And get you?

I know, it sounds silly.

—Then explain.

It's hard to explain unless you've heard some of the rumors about me.

—I haven't. Teachers, especially a teacher moonlighting

as a counselor, tend to get left out of student gossip. Not that we don't have our own gossip.

About you?

He laughs.

—It depends. What have you heard?

Nothing. I'm joking.

—But you'll tell me if you hear anything.

I promise.

Don't joke, Mr. Porter. Help her. Get back to Hannah. Please.

—When was the last time a rumor . . . popped up?

See, that's it. Not all of them are rumors.

—Okay.

No. Listen . . .

Please listen.

Years ago I was voted . . . you know, in one of those polls. Well, not really a poll, but someone's stupid idea of a list. A best-of and worst-of thing.

He doesn't respond. Did he see it? Does he know what she's talking about?

And people have been reacting to it ever since.

—When was the last time?

I hear her pull a tissue from the box.

Recently. At a party. I swear, one of the worst nights of my life.

—Because of a rumor?

So much more than a rumor. But partly, yes.

—Can I ask what happened at this party?

It wasn't really during the party. It was after.

—Okay, Hannah, can we play Twenty Questions?

What?

—Sometimes it's hard for people to open up, even to a counselor where everything is strictly confidential.

Okay.

—So, can we play Twenty Questions?

Yes.

—At this party you mentioned, are we talking about a boy?

Yes. But again, it wasn't during the party.

—I understand that. But we need to start somewhere.

Okay.

He exhales deeply.

—I'm not going to judge you, Hannah, but did anything happen that night that you regret?

Yes.

I stand up and walk to the outer bars of the rocket. Wrapping my hands around two of the bars, I touch my face to the empty space between them.

—Did anything happen with this boy—and you can be totally honest with me, Hannah—did anything happen that might be considered illegal?

You mean rape? No. I don't think so.

—Why don't you know?

Because there were circumstances.

—Alcohol?

Maybe, but not with me.

—Drugs?

No, just more circumstances.

—Are you thinking of pressing charges?

No. I'm . . . no.

I exhale a full breath of air.

—Then what are your options?

I don't know.

Tell her, Mr. Porter. Tell her what her options are.

—What can we do to solve this problem, Hannah? Together.

Nothing. It's over.

—Something needs to be done, Hannah. Something needs to change for you.

I know. But what are my options? I need you to tell me.

—Well, if you won't press charges, if you're not sure if you even can press charges, then you have two options.

What? What are they?

She sounds hopeful. She's putting too much hope in his answers.

—One, you can confront him. We can call him in here to discuss what happened at this party. I can call you both out of . . .

You said there were two options.

—Or two, and I'm not trying to be blunt here, Hannah, but you can move on.

You mean, do nothing?

I grip the bars and shut my eyes tight.

—It is an option, and that's all we're talking about. Look, something happened, Hannah. I believe you. But if you won't press charges and you won't confront him, you need to consider the possibility of moving beyond this.

And if that's not a possibility? Then what? Because guess what, Mr. Porter, she won't do it.

Move beyond this?

—Is he in your class, Hannah?

He's a senior.

—So he'll be gone next year.

You want me to move beyond this.

It's not a question, Mr. Porter. Don't take it as one. She's thinking out loud. It's not an option because she can't do it. Tell her you're going to help her.

There's a rustle.

Thank you, Mr. Porter.

No!

—Hannah. Wait. You don't need to leave.

I scream through the bars. Over the trees. "No!"

I think I'm done here.

Do not let her leave.

I got what I came for.

—I think there's more we can talk about, Hannah.

No, I think we've figured it out. I need to move on and get over it.

—Not get over it, Hannah. But sometimes there's nothing left to do but move on.

Do not let her leave that room!

You're right. I know.

—Hannah, I don't understand why you're in such a hurry to leave.

Because I need to get on with things, Mr. Porter. If nothing's going to change, then I'd better get on with it, right?

—Hannah, what are you talking about?

I'm talking about my life, Mr. Porter.

A door clicks.

—Hannah, wait.

Another click. Now the tearing of Velcro.

Footsteps. Picking up speed.

I'm walking down the hall.

Her voice is clear. It's louder.

His door is closed behind me. It's staying closed.

A pause.

He's not coming.

I press my face hard against the bars. They feel like a vise tightening against my skull the further I push.

He's letting me go.

The point behind my eyebrow is throbbing so hard, but I don't touch it. I don't rub it. I let it pound.

I think I've made myself very clear, but no one's stepping forward to stop me.

Who else, Hannah? Your parents? Me? You were not very clear with me.

A lot of you cared, just not enough. And that . . . that is what I needed to find out.

But I didn't know what you were going through, Hannah.

And I did find out.

The footsteps continue. Faster.

And I'm sorry.

The recorder clicks off.

With my face pressing against the bars, I begin to cry. If anyone is walking through the park, I know they can hear me. But I don't care if they hear me because I can't believe I just heard the last words I'll ever hear from Hannah Baker.

"I'm sorry." Once again, those were the words. And now, anytime someone says I'm sorry, I'm going to think of her.

But some of us won't be willing to say those words back. Some of us will be too angry at Hannah for killing herself and blaming everyone else.

I would have helped her if she'd only let me. I would have helped her because I want her to be alive.

The tape vibrates in the Walkman as it reaches the end of its spool.

CASSETTE 7: SIDE B

The tape clicks itself over and continues playing.

Without her voice, the slight static hum that constantly played beneath her words sounds louder. Over seven tapes and thirteen stories, her voice was kept at a slight distance by this steady hum in the background.

I let this sound wash over me as I hold onto the bars and close my eyes. The bright moon disappears. The swaying treetops disappear. The breeze against my skin, the fading pain in my fingers, the sound of this tape winding from one spool to the next, reminds me of everything I've heard over the past day.

My breathing begins to slow. The tension in my muscles starts to relax.

Then, a click in the headphones. A slow breath of air.

I open my eyes to the bright moonlight.

And Hannah, with warmth.

Thank you.

■

THE NEXT DAY
AFTER MAILING THE TAPES

I fight every muscle in my body, begging me to collapse. Begging me not to go to school. To go anywhere else and hide out till tomorrow. But no matter when I go back, the fact remains, eventually I need to face the other people on the tapes.

I approach the entrance to the parking lot, a patch of ivy with a wide slab of etched stone welcoming us back to high school. COURTESY OF THE CLASS OF '93. I've walked past this stone many times over the past three years, but not once with the parking lot this full. Not once, because I have never been this late.

Till today.

For two reasons.

One: I waited outside the post office doors. Waiting for them to open so I could mail a shoebox full of audiotapes. I used a brown paper bag and a roll of packing tape to rewrap it, conveniently forgetting to add my return address. Then I mailed the package to Jenny Kurtz, changing the way she'll see life, how she'll see the world, forever.

And two: Mr. Porter. If I sit there in first period, with him writing on the board or standing behind the podium, the only place I can imagine looking is in the middle of the room, one desk to the left.

The empty desk of Hannah Baker.

People stare at her desk every day. But today, for me, is profoundly different than yesterday. So I'll take my time at my locker. And in the restroom. Or wandering through the halls.

I follow a sidewalk that traces the outer edge of the school parking lot. I follow it across the front lawn, through the glass double doors of the main building. And it feels strange, almost sad, to walk through the empty halls. Each step I take sounds so lonely.

Behind the trophy display are five freestanding banks of lockers, with offices and restrooms on either side. I see a few other students late for school, gathering their books.

I reach my locker, lean my head forward, and rest it against the cool metal door. I concentrate on my shoulders and neck, relaxing the muscles. I concentrate on my breathing to slow it down. Then I turn the combination dial to five. Then left to four, then right to twenty-three.

How many times did I stand right here, thinking I would never get a chance with Hannah Baker?

I had no idea how she felt about me. No idea who she really was. Instead, I believed what other people said about her. And I was afraid what they might say about me if they knew I liked her.

I spin the dial, clearing the combination.

Five.

Four.

Twenty-three.

How many times after the party did I stand right here, when Hannah was still alive, thinking my chances with her were over? Thinking I said or did something wrong. Too afraid to talk to her again. Too afraid to try.

And then, when she died, the chances disappeared forever.

It all began a few weeks ago, when a map slipped through the vents of my locker.

I wonder what's in Hannah's locker right now. Is it empty? Did the custodian pack everything into a box, drop it in a storage closet, waiting for her parents to return? Or does her locker remain untouched, exactly as she left it?

With my forehead still pressed against the metal, I turn my head just enough to look into the nearest hallway, toward the always-open door to first period. Mr. Porter's room.

Right there, outside his door, is where I last saw Hannah Baker alive.

I close my eyes.

Who am I going to see today? Besides me, eight people at this school have already listened to the tapes. Eight people, today, are waiting to see what the tapes have done to me. And over the next week or so, as the tapes move on, I'll be doing the same to the rest of them.

In the distance, muffled by a classroom wall, comes a familiar voice. I slowly open my eyes. But the voice will never sound friendly again.

"I need someone to take this to the front office for me."

Mr. Porter's voice creeps down the hall straight at me. The muscles in my shoulders feel tight, heavy, and I pound my fist into the locker.

A chair squeaks, followed by footsteps leaving his room. My knees feel ready to crumble, waiting for the student to see me and ask why I'm not in class.

From a bank of lockers further up, someone clicks a locker shut.

Coming out of Mr. Porter's class, Steve Oliver nods his head at me and smiles. The student from the other locker rounds the corner into the hall, almost colliding into Steve.

She whispers, "I'm sorry," then moves around him to get by.

Steve looks down at her but doesn't respond, just keeps

up his pace, moving closer to me. "All right, Clay!" he says. Then he laughs. "Someone's late for class, huh?"

Beyond him, in the hallway, the girl turns. It's Skye.

The back of my neck starts sweating. She looks at me, and I hold her gaze for a few steps, then she turns to keep walking.

Steve walks up close, but I don't look at him. I motion for him to move to the side. "Talk to me later," I say.

Last night, on the bus, I left without talking to Skye. I wanted to talk with her, I tried to, but I let her slide out of the conversation. Over the years, she's learned how to avoid people. Everyone.

I step away from my locker and watch her continue down the hall.

I want to say something, to call her name, but my throat tightens.

Part of me wants to ignore it. To turn around and keep myself busy, doing anything, till second period.

But Skye's walking down the same stretch of hall where I watched Hannah slip away two weeks ago. On that day, Hannah disappeared into a crowd of students, allowing the tapes to say her good-bye. But I can still hear the footsteps of Skye Miller, sounding weaker and weaker the further she gets.

And I start walking, toward her.

I pass the open door to Mr. Porter's room and, in one hurried glance, pull in more than I expected. The empty desk near the center of the room. Empty for two weeks and for the rest of the year. Another desk, my desk, empty for one day. Dozens of faces turn toward me. They recognize me, but they don't see everything. And there's Mr. Porter, facing away, but starting to turn.

A flood of emotion rushes into me. Pain and anger. Sadness and pity. But most surprising of all, hope.

I keep walking.

Skye's footsteps are growing louder now. And the closer I get to her, the faster I walk, and the lighter I feel. My throat begins to relax.

Two steps behind her, I say her name.

"Skye."

13 Inspirations

JoanMarie
for saying, "I do,"
and when I almost gave up because I thought
I'd never sell a book,
for saying, "You will."

Robin Mellom & Eve Porinchak
"The road to publication is like a churro—
long and bumpy, but sweet."
You two made it sweet.
(Disco Mermaids forever!)

Mom & Dad & Nate
for encouraging my creative pursuits from the beginning
. . . no matter how ridiculous.

Laura Rennert
for saying, "I can sell this."

Kristen Pettit
for saying, "Can I buy this?"
Your editorial guidance brought this book to a whole new level.

S.L.O.W. for Children
(my critique group)
for being so critical . . . in a good way.

Lin Oliver & Stephen Mooser at SCBWI
for years of professional support and encouragement
(the Work-In-Progress grant was nice, too).

ROXYANNE YOUNG AT SMARTWRITERS.COM
for believing in this book from the beginning
(the Grand Prize designation was nice, too).

KATHLEEN DUEY
for mentoring me through the early stages of this creative pursuit.

CHRIS CRUTCHER
for writing *Stotan!*, the first teen novel I ever read.
and for encouraging me to finish this, the first teen novel
I ever wrote.

KATE O'SULLIVAN
Your excitement about this novel kept me excited
about this novel.

THE LIBRARIANS & BOOKSELLERS OF SHERIDAN,
WYOMING & SAN LUIS OBISPO, CALIFORNIA
Not just co-workers, but friends.

NANCY HURD
The reason I wrote my first book . . . thirteen years ago.

"Thank You"